He Speaks Again!

Then I hear a sound that freezes me to the spot. The sound is a voice, and the very resonance of it grabs me around the throat. Too shocked to do anything else, I sit back down with a thud.

"You okay?" asks a passing stranger, but I don't answer.

I fight against every urge to look up and see where the voice came from, but deep inside I know already, and it's too late. Too late to toss me around like this, after so many years. I look up at my brother, at Neat. Owner of a voice!

Against all reason, despite all history, he opens his mouth and speaks again.

"I want to save the world, Susan."

My head swirls and the amphitheater does flip-flops around me.

"Will you help me?"

I can't answer, I can't respond. Instead I bend down and vomit all over my shoe.

T0370209

FAT BOY
SAVES
WORLD

Ian Bone

POCKET PULSE

New York   London   Toronto   Sydney   Singapore

POCKET PULSE published by
Pocket Books, a division of Simon & Schuster, Inc.
1230 Avenue of the Americas, New York, NY 10020

Copyright © 1998 by Ian Bone

Published by arrangement with Thomas C. Lothian Pty. Ltd.
First published in Australia in 1998 by Thomas C. Lothian Pty. Ltd.

ISBN 978-1-4424-3105-8

First Pocket Pulse printing October 2001

10 9 8 7 6 5 4 3 2 1

POCKET PULSE and colophon are trademarks of
Simon & Schuster, Inc.

For information regarding special discounts for bulk purchases, please
contact Simon & Schuster Special Sales at 1-800-456-6798
or business@simonschuster.com

Cover design by Jeanne M. Lee

Printed in the U.S.A.

*For Liz
and her terracotta muses*

FAT BOY
SAVES
WORLD

1

WELCOME TO THE THEATER OF POSSIBILITY

Extract from *The Silent Boy*
by Peter Bennett, winner of the
International Peace Prize for Literature

After the last guests had gone, I crept quietly into Brian's room to "see if everything was all right." It was a useless task, really.

He didn't need me to tuck his blankets in or puff his pillow, yet somehow it gave me a sense of worth, that I was being a good father to him.

He lay sleeping, his bloated body curled up in the middle of the queen-size bed we bought for him, his mouth slightly open. Oh, that mouth, how I wished it would make a noise, let out a yelp of joy or a cry for help as it had done when he was a baby. Cute little boy he was then, picking up the world in his tiny hands and placing it in his mouth, tasting all experience, then belting out a "Ga" or a "Ba," his appraisal and summation.

Now that mouth remains shut, closed off from the world, leaving me cut off from him. Around his room were the countless little labels I had placed under anything I could identify. Light switch, doorknob, picture, dresser, bed . . . each one put there in a vain attempt to ignite a speech bubble, get my son to speak again. They were once my hope, my innovative plan of action; now they were symbols of my failure. I couldn't prompt Brian back into speech, despite my good intentions and clever ideas. There was a secret in his brain that kept his mouth shut forever, and I doubt if even Brian knew what it was.

With a quiet respect for my son's silence, I tore down the labels from his walls, screwing each one up into a tiny ball of discarded paper. And in that moment a curious and disturbing image came to me—that Brian was a terminal patient on life-support equipment; that each label I tore down was like turning off a machine, consigning him to die in peace, away from the respirators and heart monitors.

Of course, he wasn't dying.

I was giving up.

Susan

Now she's called him fat.

His great, corpulent body reduced to a three-letter word. Surely she can do better than that. What about "blubber boy," or "Ayers Rock on legs," or even "wobble guts"? Any of those insults would do justice to my brother's hard-earned mounds of flesh, his massive rolls and crevices. Still, it looks as though "fat" is going to be the funniest dart this hot-dog-stand girl will throw this morning. She just doesn't understand the power of words—she's not paid to, is she? She's paid to ask the standard "Can I help you?" question in a singsong voice. She's paid to wait for a reply, even if none comes at first, but she's not paid to wait forever. And after she'd asked her question three times of my brother she lost patience. That's when she came to the conclusion that he was "fat." Oh, and she added "stupid" as well.

Stupid he is not.

She is dedicated to her hot dogs, this hot-dog gal. You can see that by her perseverance. My brother stabs his

5

chubby finger at the row of photographs behind her, and she cranes her neck around to see which one he's pointing at. Could it be the glossy print of chili dog? Plastic-red-shiny sausage, poking limply out of a flaccid bun. Or is it good ol' cheese dog he's indicating? Covered in a pile of artificial yellow string (which doesn't convince me it's cheese). Or perhaps it's American dog, looking cheekily out of its bun? There's so many of these colored dog photographs, who can tell?

"The . . . um . . . chili dog? Is that it?" asks the hotdog girl, thinking she might have the answer. "You want the chili dog?"

My brother adjusts his stance slightly, so that he now faces the grinning customer to his left. With arm raised and fat finger poised, he continues to point insistently at the photographs, never once taking his eyes off his shoes. The girl wheels around again, scanning the photographs like she's never seen them before, then turns back to my brother's arm, just to make sure she has the right trajectory. I admire her stamina; I would have given up ages ago.

"Not the chili dog? The cheese dog, that's it," she announces triumphantly. "But you didn't want the cheese dog before."

How can she be so sure? They've only just met, and since he hasn't spoken a word to her, she must be guessing. But what else could she do? She dances the same dance with her customers every day. The three-step waltz of request, service, and payment, except they speak when they do it. I suppose I should step in now and break it up, tap him on the shoulder and move the transaction along, but I won't. It's been so long since I really looked at my big brother, since I sat back and took the time to see all of him. And I don't just mean his boiling, swinging body either. I mean the air around him, the neat, self-contained swirls that go with his every move. He is so complete—over-complete in some eyes—that he doesn't need me. And I can understand why I gave him that nickname so many years ago, and why it has stuck since. He is not Brian to me, never was a Brian. To me he is "Neat."

"Not the chili dog, not the American dog, not the cheese dog, not the Paris dog, and not the husky dog!" She's sounding very heated now.

"That's all the dogs we've got, so what the hell do you want? All of them or something?!"

There is a barely perceptible nod from Neat's head, and the girl exhales a slow expletive.

"Bloody hell, he wants all of them. Okay, I hope you've got the money . . ."

A twenty-dollar note appears from nowhere, squeezed between Neat's fingers, and she snatches it. With wisps of blond hair falling over her face, the hotdog girl sets about making the dogs, their color photographs leering at her from the wall. And if photographs could laugh, they'd be drying their eyes by now.

We sit on a slatted wooden bench, and Neat devours his lunch, one dog at a time in two great bites. He eats and I watch. The cheese dog goes down in a screaming heap, the chili dog puts up a bit of a fight but succumbs in the end. American dog is about to be silently put down when an elderly woman approaches us from the bench opposite. She wears sensible walking shoes and a wide straw hat, which casts a dark shadow over her face.

"That's amazing," she says, indicating the flecks of plastic cheese splattered across Neat's vast stomach. "I sat there, you know, and I said to myself, 'Is this some sort of act?' You know, one of those buskers? They're all so sophisticated these days. But he's not, is he? He really did eat them. It's a pity my husband wasn't here to see it, he would have enjoyed it so much. Thank you." She shakes my hand.

"It was nothing," I hear myself say, too stunned to think of any witty reply. When I look up again the woman has already departed, on her way to another bench to see another show.

"What a joke," I say to Neat. "She thinks you're some kind of busker. Ha! Fat Boy Eats Dogs in Middle of City! How embarrassing."

He doesn't think it's embarrassing—at least I don't think he does. He doesn't blush, just picks up bits of cheese that have fallen onto his royal blue, little-boy shirt from the hot dogs. God, the color of that shirt is so bad, he can't have been dressed by my mother. She'd rather be dead than commit such a crime against good taste. It must have been that dippy German girl I ran into at my parents' house. "I am friend of family . . . nanny . . . you see?"

I've always hated that word "nanny" — it sounds like a little kid trying to say "Nancy." And why the hell did Neat need a nanny, anyway? Mother and Father weren't around to ask, all I had was the nanny. I suppose I could have asked her, but I was too busy having fun.

I threw my bags onto the marble floor and took in the air-conditioned atmosphere of my parents' luxury.

The nanny watched me like I was a thief. "Yes, yes. Who you are, please?" She was tall, thin, blond, and beautiful, but I tried not to hate her for that. She stood with her arms folded, smelling like something very expensive. Smelling just like my mother's Parisian perfumes!

"Please, you are?" she asked in a thick German accent.

"Yes," I answered.

She rocked back on her sensible flat-soled shoes and blinked, nonplussed by my reply.

"I am pleased," I explained. "Are you?"

"No, no, not please. Verena, my name is Verena."

That's when I got the "friend of family nanny" routine—about her daddy in Germany, author and friend of famous Australian author, my father. It all blended into blah blah blah after a while, so I breezed into the kitchen for some light relief. There was a fat sausage lurking inside my parents' fridge, winking at me. I winked back. Verena followed me, continuing her breathy interrogation in my ear.

"So, who your name is?" she asked.

"It's Susan," I replied. "The long-lost daughter. I ran away to the circus when I was twelve, and I've decided to come back."

Most of my joke was lost in the translation, but she did manage to pick up my name.

"Oh no, no," she snorted. "Susan has hair down here." She indicated her shoulders, and I rubbed my hand over my recently shaved scalp, the stubble so soft and prickly.

"Yeah, well," I said. "I shaved it as a statement."

"Good," she said. "Look good."

"Bull." I laughed. "I look like a cancer patient. Susan Bennett, sporting the latest look in chemotherapy chic."

I did a twirl for her and she laughed.

"So, you are home now?" she asked.

"Looks like it," I said.

Verena laughed again, all the way out of the kitchen, down the hall, and through the front door. Perhaps she was just taking a stroll to clear her mind, or maybe she went to buy an English/German dictionary. Then she could look up "chic," and "chemotherapy." I caught a glimpse of my bald head in the polished chrome of the upright freezer. What was German for "stupid"? I wondered. An idiot like me, who gets sucked in by her own hype? Who thinks she's making a radical statement, a real jab in the eye to the sweethearts around her, only to find out they didn't give a stuff? It would be a long word, wouldn't it, to cover something like that? And perhaps there'd be a pithy German phrase for the confusion I felt when they called me in for a "friendly chat." My dear boarding-school teachers, watching me sit stiffly in their leather armchairs as they suggested I take a bit of a holiday: "Go home for a while and think about your life." And for a moment I thought they were joking. I tried to sound cool and witty; I even laughed, saying, "Good one." But they didn't laugh. Next thing I knew I was homeward bound on the train, wondering if I'd won the battle or lost the war. No one wished me goodbye at the station, no one rushed out of their room to beg me to stay.

I found a hard-boiled egg hiding behind the sausage and sprinkled it with salt. It looked as if my mother wasn't home, and I was going to need plenty of fortification to face her good taste. At least at school I didn't have to put up with her expensive artistic flair, *occupying the surfaces, the spaces, the definitions between void and object* . . . Like the disgusting sculpture that stood at the bottom of the stairs. All wire, wood, and iron; another crappy piece of art by a struggling artist from my mother's gallery.

My mother takes these people under her wing, organizing exhibitions and publicity for them until it becomes painfully obvious that they won't ever make it. Then she drops them. Boom! Just like that. "Bye-bye, have a nice career . . . not."

I went up to my mother's bedroom. It hadn't changed. The finely carved wooden bed so neatly made, tasteful sheets tucked in hospital-tight. A wooden picture frame on the dresser next to her bed showing two happy little children squeezed into oval and square shapes. I picked it up and stared at these strangers. Little Susan and her big brother, Brian, the children my mother wanted to have. Look at the smile on Susan's face. The toothy, wide-open innocence of it that was wiped out on my eighth birthday when my brother stopped talking. Where does a smile go? I don't mean the physical pulling of muscles around the mouth, but the joy that speaks through the eyes? My eyes. I did smile again after that day, but who was I trying to kid? Certainly not my mother. She packed away the camera, put the photo frames in her bottom drawer, and bought herself an art gallery.

My life went on without photographs. No shots of ten-year-old Susan, hair in a ponytail, sporting a gappy-toothed grin as she plays spies with her cuddly bear brother. Sitting him down on the living room carpet, talking through the plot in a machine-gun string of falsetto monologue. "Quick, Neat! The canister of nerve gas! Release it now! Yes. Yes, they're all dead." Holding his arm up in a victory salute, letting it flop to his side, then running out the back on another adventure. Neat, left alone on the rug like a giant rubber doll, waiting for nothing. And every move watched. Every piece of action recorded in my father's little notebook. There are no pictures of twelve-year-old Susan as she finally realizes she does not live in an ordinary family. Making up pathetic excuses to stop my friends from coming over to my house. No pictures of fourteen-year-old Susan, packing her bags for boarding school, Neat sitting silently in my room, watching. And there won't be a photograph of today, sixteen-year-old Susan making her triumphant return. A spontaneous pose of me rubbing my stubbly head in Neat's ample tummy.

I put the photo down and drew in a deep breath—the time had come to see him. I knew where he'd be, in his bedroom. An almost bare space except for the ever-present TV set in the corner, blinking out a daytime talk show with the volume turned down. No pictures on the walls, no knickknacks scattered on his dresser to indicate his likes or dislikes. That's how his room has been for as long as I can remember. As if my mother, who stuffed my room with every imaginable piece of art and finery you could find, was punishing Neat for his state of mind. This was a room of neglected hope, this was where my brother spent most of his life. Neat sat at the end of his bed, back to the TV, elbows resting on his tummy, eyes a million miles away. In that breath between seeing him and stepping into his room, I paused. For a mere second I stopped to look at him through the eyes of Susan, a young girl who loved her cuddly-bear brother. And what I had assumed was vacant turned out to be a study of concentration. And the object of his concentrated study was a string of tiny ants, energetic and disciplined as they marched along a predetermined path on my brother's bedroom wall. He was so graceful in his pose, so contained, that I wanted to hug him, to kiss him and say I loved him. Instead I did the decent thing and walked up to his bed quietly, saying a gentle "hello." I asked him if he wanted to come with me to the city. He didn't answer, just stood and walked toward the door. That looked like a yes to me. I searched the house for Verena but she'd vanished. Dictionaries must be hard to find these days.

"You still hungry?" I ask Neat as the last hot dog goes down. He doesn't answer. All around us the city shoppers continue their single-file dance. More ants. We must look strange, the two of us, so motionless in the middle of it all. Bald girl and fat boy, liberator and liberated, one hungry the other not.

I've never done this before, never taken Neat out on

my own. He's usually so protected . . . well, protected from me at least. I have a bad reputation with my parents. No doubt it's going to hit the fan when I take him back home. So what else is new?

Why are you out of school so early? That's Father's voice, trying to sound like he's in charge.

My God! What have you done to your hair? That's Mother, experiencing aesthetic shock at the way I've butchered my "good looks."

Then the killer. *What the hell do you think you're doing? Taking your brother out like that! For God's sake, Susan, we don't want any more trouble!* That could be both of them, trembling with fright as they wonder what the Demon Sister is going to do next.

It's like one of those corny American movies, isn't it? By the light of the full moon, sweet little sister Susan transforms into an ugly monster, the Demon Sister. Fangs dripping with poisonous hate, claws that can tear you apart, she snatches the defenseless fat boy from his sanctuary and runs off into the night, her maniacal laughter echoing down the cobbled laneways. My parents run frantically from their stately home, a silver-encrusted shotgun in Father's hands. He shouts, "Put the boy down or we shoot!" But they don't wait for a response. Father raises the gun and fires. It's a miss! He shoots again and the Demon Sister roars with pain, a wounded animal, then tosses the fat boy aside. There I lie, dying in the gutter, framed in a poignant close-up. Two pairs of feet approach. Father raises the gun to finish me off, but Mother says, "No, Peter, look." And slowly my face changes back to Susan. "She used to be a sweet girl," says Mother as the last wave of life ebbs from my body. "I don't understand what happened."

This vast crowd of city shoppers should be weeping their eyes out by now, but I don't think they appreciate true melodrama.

My only accompaniment is a drum, beating in the distance, and for a moment I think the soundtrack to my corny movie is still echoing in my head. But it's just a busker or something like that, trying to entertain the masses. Instinctively, I stand, drawn to the noise. Neat stands too, and our eyes meet for a brief moment. Then he looks over my shoulder to where the drumming is coming from. It's funny that he should be attracted by noise, my silent big brother. He's resisted it for as long as I can remember, hiding behind his great wall of silence. Feeble little sisters like me have to guess what's going on in his head. I touch his sleeve and he turns toward the drumming, toward the noise. We stroll down the city mall together, brother and sister, taken in by the promise of a drumbeat.

Todd

He witnessed an accident at a busy intersection on the same day that he met the fat boy. Two stories plucked from the city, two dramatic journeys, each with its own rhythm.

Todd was waiting at the pedestrian crossing, no more than three yards away, when the car hit the girl. In the split-second gap between the squeal of brakes and the first, sickening thud of impact, he felt his heart leap against his ribs like a caged animal. The sound resonated in his head, repeating slowly, a monotonous drumbeat.

Thud!

The girl, no older than thirteen, the same age as his younger sister, just meandering across the road.

Thud!

The car, sliding in so smoothly, flipping her young body into the air.

Thud!

The windscreen a craze of smashed glass as the girl pushes it in with her back.

Thud!

Her colored backpack spinning wildly away, almost waving goodbye to its owner as she rolls onto the roof of the car.

Thud!

The hard asphalt of the road, so ungiving, receiving her cruelly, allowing her to land like a discarded doll, flopping and bouncing once, twice, until she was still.

She lay there motionless, her body twisted and seemingly broken. Todd let go of his breath and chaos erupted on the intersection's stage.

A woman's voice screamed: "Call an ambulance!" A running man holding a baby dodged traffic to come to the girl's aid. The baby's head jerked forward as the man knelt down beside the injured girl. The dented car rolled away in the background. The driver flung his hands up before his eyes in a delayed reaction to the impact. Two women ran into the scene from different angles, their arms out wide, like birds coming in to land.

Todd watched this from the side of the road, a frozen spectator, waiting for something . . . for what? An answer perhaps. Is she dead, is she alive? The climax.

Then, a flutter of magic.

The girl rolled over onto her stomach, raising herself to her knees before standing unsteadily. She was crying and holding on to the man for support.

"You made it," whispered Todd. Overcome with emotion, he rushed to her side. He had to touch her, to confirm it was real. Brushing lightly against her sleeve, under the pretense of helping her across the road, Todd mirrored her every step. He wasn't needed, the girl was leaning heavily against the man, but he had to be there. The baby reached out and touched the girl on the side of her head, flexing its tiny fingers around her cheek. The two women appeared at the girl's side and took over from the man, guiding their "patient" into a shop where they sat her down in a chair. Todd stood at the doorway of the shop and watched the girl, her arms clutched tightly around her stomach, her sobs coming in short bursts. He wrapped his own arms around his middle, holding in the emotions that threatened to explode within him. The driver rushed in, an elderly man, shaking visibly.

"How is she?" he asked. "Is she all right?" As if he couldn't believe the evidence of his own eyes.

How could she be alive? After such an impact? The simple fact of her survival brought tears to Todd's eyes. Release. An exhilarating feeling rose from his belly to his throat. This was life he was witnessing. He had an urge to hug somebody, and for the first time since he'd moved to the city, he wished his family were here. Not his hard, leathery parents, but his brothers and sister, slow-talking country kids, as young as this miracle girl. He'd grab them all, wrestle them to the ground, and laugh until he was hoarse. They'd look at him sideways —"Todd the weirdo" at it again, gone even more stupid since he ran off to the city on his seventeenth birthday. "The city is tough, the city is ungiving."

They were wrong and they would always be wrong. The city gave plenty if you knew how to take it. And Todd had learned quickly. You had to be down in the midst of it with both eyes open, ready for your chance. Ready to take the risk and swallow the magic pill. To feel the rush, be swept along on its amazing ride. To come down hard, wanting more and more. To wait for the next moment when the crazy graffiti of city life would fill you up again, make your body buzz with excitement. Like the incredible rip he got out of watching that girl get up and walk away.

An urgent wail announced the ambulance's arrival, its flashing red light very businesslike. Time to go. Todd didn't want the mundane nature of accident-scene procedures to bring him down.

Besides, he was late for the performance.

Susan

We arrive at a small amphitheater, which is cut into the ground with rows of steps acting as seats for the lunch-time audience. A red silk screen is set up in the middle of the stage area, the words Theater of Possibility pinned across the top. Four young people in colored clothing are walking around in front of the silk curtain, pointing out members of the audience and shouting out greetings.

"Hello!"

A giggle for a reply.

"G'day there."

A brief nod of the head, then a quick, embarrassed turn away.

The actors, two boys and two girls, don't seem to be bothered by the embarrassed responses their greetings bring. To the left of the curtain is a girl. She's beating the drum that Neat and I heard earlier. We sit on one of the stone steps and watch. The drumming stops, one of the actors throws the silk curtain wide open, and out steps a woman in the wildest jacket I have ever seen. She surveys the crowd with such a calm presence that I immediately want to be just like her. So self-assured and steady. The actors line up behind her, and she throws her arms wide.

"Welcome to the Theater of Possibility . . ." she booms.

What the hell have we got here?

The Coat slowly pans her eyes across the crowd, like she's taking in every facial detail, every raised eyebrow or cynical glance, before stopping at my brother. Then she says in a barely audible voice: ". . . where your wildest dreams come true."

God, if only that was true. The Coat strides to the front of the stage area and introduces the idea of the performance. The audience have to write down on a piece of paper what they have secretly always wanted to do or be, then these guys act it out on the spot. Should be a laugh.

The actors move about handing out pieces of paper and when I get mine I write "assassin," then I decide they might need a bit more information, so I add, "to kill someone famous." I guarantee they won't do that one. Neat has folded his piece of paper into a square, so I take it from him and shuffle it under mine. As I wait for one of the actors to gather the wildest dreams up, a ridiculous thought comes to me. What if Neat wrote on his paper? As far back as I can remember he hasn't spoken, but has he ever written anything down? His paper is there, nestled under mine, daring me to look, but I'm too chicken. I don't know what I'd do if it actually did have writing on it. It's such a ridiculous thought—he can't write, he can't speak, he can't do anything! And then I laugh, because they got me, didn't they? With their drumbeats and colored clothes and theatrical tricks, they got me to hope for something wilder than my wildest dream.

A voice breaks into my reverie, "Got your paper?" and I jump. It's one of the colorful boys with shockingly cute eyes. He nods to the dreams in my lap, and I hand them to him. He unfolds Neat's paper and shuffles it into the stack of other dreams. I gasp. Writing! There really was writing on Neat's paper. I call out to the actor but he's on his way down to the stage.

"I need that one back," I shout.

He shakes his head and grins over his shoulder. "No way, coward!"

"Please," I beg, but he's gone.

The show starts but it's just a blur of color and sound from some distant place. Neat shuffles next to me and I glance sideways at him. He's watching like he watched those ants, so I turn back and pay attention myself. Maybe this is Neat's dream they're acting out. The actress in red is swirling around the amphitheater saying, "I'm in love with the richest guy in the world." Turns out to be about a girl wanting to marry someone with millions of dollars. So predictable. I doubt if it's Neat's dream, but then, who knows? Perhaps his secret desire is to be a bride and wear a white princess dress, yards of satin and silk covering his corpulent flesh. To have a groom lift the veil for the kiss, only to be confronted by a pouting boy with enormous lips.

I can't stop giggling and the guy next to me hisses, "shut up," so I take deep breaths, trying to concentrate. These dreams aren't wild at all, they're just crap like getting married, making money, driving a flashy car that's bigger than your ego. The woman in the coat reaches dramatically into a hat and draws out the last dream. Perhaps this will be Neat's. I watch him carefully to see if he has any reaction when it's read out.

"And finally —" shouts the Coat, "ah, this is a good one—to be an assassin and kill someone famous."

Why did I write that? The heat rushes up my neck and I put my hands up to cover my beet-red complexion. I've got to get out of here. I nudge Neat and whisper it's time to go, but he doesn't move. Either that's a "no" or he didn't feel my nudge. Either way I have to suffer the humiliation of watching them do my pathetic attempt at humor.

The cute boy has been crowned with a silk scarf and the others are milling around him, pretending to take photographs or asking for an autograph. The music is grand, a fanfare playing from the electronic keyboard, but suddenly it changes. A low, menacing drumbeat creeps into the scene, changing the mood, and the admirers melt into the background. Now a dark figure, draped in black silk, crawls behind the famous man. He waves to the crowd, oblivious of danger. God, what an idiot, can't he see what's coming? So caught up in his little ego, he doesn't even notice that death is knocking. The black-clad figure stands as one of the actors speaks in a voice of doom: "Beware! Beware the shadow of death."

But the idiot isn't listening. He's so caught up in his little ego trip that he doesn't realize he's going to cop it. He is exposed to the menace, vulnerable to the inevitable blow. It's coming now, the dark figure so close, almost there, the raised arm, it quivers, then flashes. Down comes death, and music explodes from the tiny speakers as the actors scream. Down comes death, and the famous man crumples. A wailing chorus of admirers and fans throw themselves to the ground, weeping for his memory. I don't feel sad, I don't feel elated either, just a sort of curious feeling, like I'm rushing into something bad.

The amphitheater explodes with applause as the actors take a bow, announcing that they will be back tomorrow for another performance of the Theatre of Possibility. It takes seconds, minutes, hours for the crowd to disperse. I don't know, I'm stuck in my spot, oddly disturbed by the images I have seen.

God, it was just a stupid show.

I turn to Neat, who hasn't altered his position for the past half hour, and tap him on the shoulder.

"This time we really have to go," I say.

But still he doesn't move, as though he's waiting for something from me.

"They didn't do your dream, eh?" I find myself saying, and Neat stands.

So that was the key. I stand too and shake my legs, my head spinning slightly. Must have been sitting down for too long. I take a couple of breaths to sort myself out, the sickly feeling still clutching my guts. Then I hear a sound that freezes me to the spot. The sound is a voice, and the very resonance of it grabs me around the throat. Too shocked to do anything else, I sit back down with a thud.

"You okay?" asks a passing stranger, but I don't answer.

I fight against every urge to look up and see where the voice came from, but deep inside I know already, and it's too late. Too late to toss me around like this, after so many years. I look up at my brother, at Neat. Owner of a voice!

Against all reason, despite all history, he opens his mouth and speaks again.

"I want to save the world, Susan."

My head swirls and the amphitheater does flip-flops around me.

"Will you help me?"

I can't answer, I can't respond. Instead I bend down and vomit all over my shoe.

Todd

The troupe were doing the pre-show rehearsal when Todd arrived at the amphitheater. He put his bag down under the Theater of Possibility sign and joined in.

"You're late," said Carrie, not even bothering to meet his eyes.

Todd grunted, then took his place with the others as they practiced their improvisation skills, warming up their imaginations as well as their bodies.

Natalie told about a moment waiting at the bus stop next to a man who was carefully picking his nose. Then Tom, chosen by Natalie, sat on a box and did an exaggerated version of the nose-picking passenger. The rest of the troupe gathered behind Tom, forming a chorus that would echo Natalie's innermost thoughts.

"Gross," whispered one.

"Utterly gross," added another.

The chorus picked up the chant. "Utterly gross! Utterly gross!" louder and louder, then they froze.

Todd leaned forward. "But I wonder what it tastes like?" he said.

Now the chorus followed Todd's lead.

"Is it nice?" . . . "Is it good?" . . . "Can I have some?"

Carrie clapped her hands to signal that the drama should end there.

"Who's got another moment to use?" she asked, staring directly at Todd, who looked down at his feet.

The image of the girl lying on the road flashed through his mind, and he wrapped himself around it.

Normally he would be the first to have his hand up. "Mr. Enthusiasm," always ready with a funny story from his travels around the city. But not this one. The thought of telling this one made him feel raw, exposed, as if he would be revealing a secret inner part of himself. Someone else offered a moment, and Todd joined the chorus distractedly, only half paying attention to the drama. The sight of the girl on the road kept coming back to him, so motionless, so hurt.

So lonely.

Picked up by strange hands, comforted by strange voices. Despite the evidence of her survival, the miracle of her rising, it was the image of stillness that stayed in his mind.

Carrie gave the fifteen-minute call, and Todd went to sit by himself. He caught a flicker of bright color out of the corner of his eye, and Carrie sat down beside him wearing her bright "ringmaster" coat. The first time he'd called her that, she'd punched him on the arm before suggesting they go to the pub for a few beers.

"What happened to you today?" asked Carrie, hands in her coat pockets.

"I saw an accident," mumbled Todd.

"Yeah? Bad one?"

He shrugged and Carrie sighed.

"You seem really closed off, Todd. You gonna be okay?"

"Yes. Of course," he snapped.

"It's okay to feel shaken after witnessing an accident," said Carrie.

"I didn't feel shaken," insisted Todd. "I felt . . . I felt

good. Fantastic, even. God! This girl was knocked from here to hell and back, and she gets up and walks away. I mean, how amazing is that?"

"But you don't feel amazing now?"

"I just told you I didn't."

"Look," said Carrie in her calm, director's voice. "I don't know what happened, neither do the others, but if you don't talk about it, how can we help you?"

"There's nothing to talk about," said Todd. "I just . . . I don't know. I felt good, now I don't." He shrugged.

Carrie stood and placed a hand on Todd's shoulder. "Don't try so hard," she said quietly. Then she was gone.

Don't try so hard. That almost made him laugh. Back home it had always been the opposite message. "Get off your lazy arse and help around the farm instead of swanning around with this drama rubbish." Try hard, Todd! Try hard to be the son we want, instead of this actor weirdo. And the more they pushed him, the more he escaped to the world of theater. He swallowed all the drama his school could offer, grabbed every moment until drama became his oxygen and the dusty air of his parents' farm a poison. Then he ran away.

The beating of Natalie's drum snapped him back to the here and now. He wandered over to the drummer, her arms flashing in a blur of rhythm. Todd shook his head from side to side, then drew in a deep breath. The animal growl of the drum relaxed him, filled him with a familiar desire. To act, to stand out in a crowd of strangers and play the fool. The lunchtime shoppers took their seats, forming a loosely scattered audience, and Todd strode to the front of the stage area.

Might as well throw myself in, he thought. A woman sat down with a toddler, and Todd called out "Hello!" She looked around to make sure Todd was addressing her, then raised her hand in a halfhearted gesture of greeting. Todd grinned widely, a cheeky mood overtaking his gloom, and clapped his hands in time to the beat.

"G'day," he called out to a suited office worker.

The man looked down in embarrassment.

"Good afternoon," said Todd to the woman behind the office worker. She smiled quickly, then turned around to continue a conversation.

The other actors in the troupe walked to the front of the stage, grins on their faces, and stood next to Todd.

"What are you doing?" asked Tom.

"Just being friendly." Todd laughed.

He waved wildly to a group of young women and they waved back. The others shrugged, then started greeting the audience too, warming to the role with each hello. Todd felt his shoulders loosen up, and he shouted, loudly, "Well, hello!"

A dancing, Pan-like creature squeezed and pushed its way into his skin, twisting his face into a smile, puffing his chest out to full size. He was the trickster, the wild card, the prancer full of confidence and vitality.

The crowd had built up considerably now, and Natalie stopped the drumbeat. Todd took his position with the other actors as Carrie walked out, giving her dramatic introduction.

"Welcome to the Theater of Possibility, where your wildest dreams come true."

The rest of the introduction went like a blur, until it was time to hand out the pieces of paper. As Todd passed Carrie, she gave him a quizzical look.

She liked it, thought Todd. It was wild but it worked.

The performance didn't quite match the pace of the drumbeat opening. The first story was about getting married, and the rest followed the same predictable path. Todd felt his energy dissipating. It was hard to keep the enthusiasm up when the stories were boring. Then Carrie pulled out the final story, the assassination of a famous man, and Todd's eyes lit up. In the group huddle he begged to have the role of the famous man, and the others nodded. If he was so warmed up to that role, then it was his.

Todd took one of the silk scarves they used for props and wrapped it around his head like a crown. He strode out onto the stage, smooth and complete. Clare and Tom flanked him, forming a chorus to sing the praises of the famous man. They filled him with majestic words, with adoring voices, and the character grew, stretching into the empty spaces within Todd. He rose up and filled the amphitheater, towering high above the buildings. Untouched by human sorrow, unfazed by human fear. The actor and the character completely merged, floating in a trance of invincibility. And yes, Todd felt the same exhilaration as this morning, rekindled the flame of joy at the sight of a young girl rising from the road.

What a rush! He was flying in the character. *Bring on the climax, let it happen.* The menace in Natalie's drumbeat heightened his senses further. *Come on! Come on!*

When the "blow" finally came he was released. At last, this was the end, the final moment. He lay on the ground, betrayed, shattered and broken. Dead.

The audience clapped.

Susan

Vomiting is such an honest reaction, not a hint of social nicety or "doing the right thing" about it. It is sheer, up-front, out-of-ya-face truth.

I sit on the stone steps and try to regain my composure. There can be precious little left in my stomach, but God knows what will happen if Neat decides to speak again. As my breathing slowly returns to calm, a new sensation comes over me. I feel intensely embarrassed, not because of the mess all over my shoe either. Have I missed something? Did the whole world know that Neat was talking again except for me? Perhaps it was in one of Mother's letters. *The gallery is going well, the rosebushes are blooming, and by the way, Brian has started talking again* . . . No! She would have called me, Father would have written about it, for Christ's sake!

I look up at my talking teddy bear. He has his back to me, staring at the actors as they pack away their makeshift theater, and I decide to risk another attack by asking him a question.

"How long have you been able to talk?"

But he ignores my question, concentrating all his attention on the busy actors. Perhaps he didn't really speak, after all. But there is such irrefutable evidence all over the concrete steps that I don't doubt what I heard.

"For Christ's sake," I yelp. "Don't tell me you're gonna stop talking again."

"Fat boy saves world," says Neat flatly.

Ah! The sound that only minutes ago brought me terror now fills me with awe. His voice, deeper than I would ever have imagined. It comes from way back, a place buried down in his throat, traveling up through rolls of fat and flesh to be heard by me. To be witnessed.

He ambles over to the actors and stands conspicuously among them as they try to pack away their silk screen. I quickly wipe the mess from my shoe and join him. The actors' only exit is blocked by Neat's bulk.

"Excuse me, mate," says the cute boy who took our "dreams."

Neat ignores his request, standing stock-still, making a statement with his presence. The actors put the frame down and place their hands on their hips.

"Look, pal, what's the problem?" says another.

"Come on," I say to Neat, my head still swimming in an imaginary sea. "They've got to pack up."

He doesn't move.

"Is he okay?" asks the cute boy.

"Of course he's okay," I snap. "He's just disappointed, that's all. He wanted you to do his dream thing."

"Oh, well"—the boy grins—"we'll be back tomorrow. He can try then."

"You hear that, Neat? You can try tomorrow."

"Neat?" says the cute one. "Is that his name? I like it. He looks like a Neat."

I look at the actor sideways. Does he really mean that or is he spinning a line? He seems genuine, even walks up to Neat and shakes his hand.

"Hi, I'm Todd," he says. "Tell you what you should do. Come back and see us, same time tomorrow, okay? Make sure you give your piece of paper to me, understand? We'll see what we can do."

Neat regards him for a few seconds, as if he's pondering the offer, then walks away.

"I think that means okay," I explain breathlessly, rushing after him.

The actors continue to pack up as I take Neat's hand. "This time, we are definitely going home," I say.

There's a fountain in the middle of the mall, and I throw my shoe into the water, ignoring the looks of passing strangers. Neat quietly watches me, a strange look on his face, almost a smile. So what's so unusual about this? I'm washing vomit off my shoe in the middle of the city with my brother—the one that wants to save the world. And why not? When you look at the world through Neat's eyes, it sure does need saving. Yeah, you save the bloody world if you can, my roly-poly boy. Save me while you're at it, God knows I could do with it, too.

We board a bus for home and I squeeze into the window seat, crushed by the stiff bulk of my would-be savior, his arms out straight as he holds on to the railing of the seat in front.

The shock catches up with me now, and my heart

starts to sprint like an Olympian. I want to slow it down, every crappy aspect of my life, just make it stop! But I can't do that, not the way Neat did eight years ago. I'm not strong like him. I have to keep going even when it's falling apart around me. I have to fight all the way, kicking and scratching at anything that moves. Him, he just decided to turn off the gas on my eighth birthday. And it didn't matter how many doctors my father took him to, he remained silent. So my father stopped paying doctor's bills and started writing. He turned his son's illness into a smart career move by publishing *The Silent Boy*. Not so silent now, is he?

The bus arrives at our stop, and Neat takes hours to waddle down the steps. We finally hit the footpath and make our way home. There are packed bags in the foyer, Verena's packed bags. She bustles out of the dining room in a flurry of movement and squeals with shock at the sight of us.

"Oh, you return. Well, yes, good. I go now, thank you."

"For what?" I ask.

"Hmm?"

"What are you thanking me for?"

"You are home for the boy, yes?"

"I'm home for me, thanks."

"Oh, you are joker," she says, picking up her suitcases.

"Where's my mother? Does she know you're going?"

"Hmm?" Verena sighs, putting her suitcases back on the ground.

"My mother. *Mutter?*"

"Oh, gone. They overseas now, hmm . . . father and mother. Geneva. Frankfurt."

I let out a sigh too, my last gasp of air escaping me. I hadn't banked on that one coming. Okay, so no parental dramas, no stern looks from Father and shocked expressions from Mother. No news of the talking brother, either. Just this flitty "nanny," a so-called friend of the family, making off with my mother's perfume.

The "nanny" picks up her suitcases for the last time, and a wild and wicked mood overtakes me. I can't possibly let dear Nanny leave without a little souvenir. One of Mother's prized pieces of artwork, a glass and bronze statue, sits on the hall table. I grab it by the legs and shove its ugly head under Verena's arm.

"Here," I pant, "a little present from Mutter."

There must be dozens of other things that my mother could donate. This tasteful little silver ashtray, for instance. Another one of my mother's favorites. I balance it on top of the largest suitcase, ignoring Nanny's red-faced plea. A grotesque lamp of glass and bronze stands on a nearby antique table, so I unplug it and shove it under Nanny's free arm. My next victim is a horrible little painting, all gloom and doom, by one of my mother's "boys." I wedge that between the large suitcase and Nanny's petite thighs.

"No, please," begs Verena. "Nein, nein."

Now Neat takes a step forward, a silver candlestick raised menacingly in his hand.

"*Mein Gott!*" screams his nanny. "*Nein.*"

She opens her mouth to scream again, and Neat carefully places the candlestick sideways between her teeth, like a Spanish rose. She almost looks jaunty, staggering backward out the door, abusing us in muffled German. I'd love to call out *auf wiedersehen* to her, wave a white lacy handkerchief, but I'm bent double with laughter. Farewell my lovely, my little German Fraülein. May you dream of fat boys and candlesticks and Parisian perfumes. I turn to my coconspirator to share the joke, but he's vanished. Melted back into the oak and marble, done a runner like the departing nanny. I suddenly feel cold.

Father's drinks cabinet looks lonely, so I tell it all about my day as I pour a Scotch. Too much has happened today, too many turns and twists, too many voices and not enough explanations. It's the leather lounge's turn to listen now, but it doesn't seem interested. In fact, none of my parents' immaculate decor could give a stuff about my day. It probably has no idea who I am. This auspicious home was once my battleground—the scene of my rebellion. Susan Bennett, freedom fighter, champion of the oppressed. Well, two oppressed at least, and only one of us could speak. I had to be doubly loud. I had to fight doubly hard and long for my damaged brother and for my damaged life. Then they exiled me to boarding-school hell, and now when I come back all the rules have changed. I wonder what my role in the family is now? The tired old heroine without a battle to fight.

I toss my shot glass of Scotch into the marble fireplace, just for the hell of it. As a sort of punctuation, I suppose, or perhaps I'm expressing myself.

"I'm not ready!" That's what I should shout. "I'm not ready to give in. The war isn't over yet!"

Todd

He twisted the key in the rusted lock, exhausted and drained. The corridor was cast in its usual gloom. This was home. A run-down boardinghouse with rotting carpets and smudged brown doors that were never opened. The only bright features about the place were the gold numbers on each of the doors. The rest was falling apart, either rapidly or slowly. He used to love this place, was delighted the first morning he arrived by the way the landlord had to fight to turn the key in the rusted lock. And the smell of rising damp that assaulted his senses when he first entered his room was perfect.

"Just needs a bit of airing," the landlord had said confidently, opening the window. But there was no insect screen and the tiny room quickly filled with flies, so Todd had closed the window again.

"If you need anything, I'm just around the corner," grumbled the landlord, giving clear messages with his eyes that he was not to be bothered.

Todd had sat on his single bed that morning in his new room, so small and dim and smelly, and seen only wide open spaces. He had finally escaped prison, escaped the constant pressure to conform to life on his parents' farm. He was in the land of the free, a run-down boardinghouse with filthy brown doors. And behind each of those doors was a character out of his wildest fantasy, a source of rich entertainment.

There was the "moaner" from room number one.

Todd had only seen him a couple of times—a painfully thin, gray-haired shadow of a man who had a disturbingly familiar face. The "whistler" from number two—a young man who spent most of his time alone in the room playing songs on a guitar and whistling loudly. His music was almost demented in its relentless cheer, yet the whistler from number two had a sad face. The "lovers" from number five—an old woman and her young boyfriend. They tried to pass as mother and son, but he was dark and swarthy and she was pale. Todd had caught glimpses of quick little kisses as their door was closing. The "bottlo" in number seven who spent all day and all night drinking bottles of beer, then rolling them around his room. And the TV freak from room eight, where the only sign of life was the blue glow from the TV under the door.

Pick-a-freak—that was the game Todd played here. Shuffle down the gloomy hallway, scuff your feet on the rotting carpet until a brown door opened and presented a peek show. Then enjoy the delicious moments, like walking in on the old woman and her young friend in the kitchen one day. They were holding hands, relaxed, but quickly sat upright when Todd intruded. The air was thick with electric questions. *Does he know? What are they doing? Did the kid see us? Were they holding hands?* This was his private theater of the bizarre, his corridor of weirdness. He stole each little moment for himself, presenting them eagerly to his theater friends, as if he could grow stronger with the telling of each story. They didn't hear the edge of despair in Todd's laugh as he recounted the antics of his neighbors. They didn't see the look in their friend's eyes as he finished a freak-show story. They were too busy bending double with laughter or being blinded with wide-eyed wonder.

Todd shut the front door of the boardinghouse with a loud bang and waited for a response. Nothing came, except perhaps a faint whiff of something going off from the kitchen. He decided to walk quickly up the corridor today, hoping not to hear a moan from number one or a whistle from number two. He made it to his door and fought with the lock until it opened. Inside, the bare furnishings hung like neglected rags in an op shop. Todd lay down on his thin foam mattress and stared at the cracks in the ceiling.

He tried to think about today's performance, but his mind kept drifting away, relaxing into a half-sleep. Car accidents and Carrie's coat and famous men and shouting "G'day" merged into a gentle mush. Then the sight of the fat boy, so large and immovable, spat out of his half-dream, and he woke up. He could see the fat boy's face, see it in sharp focus, so flabby but so strong. Todd recognized something in the fat kid's eyes. Desire. That was it. The fat kid wanted to see his story performed so much that it ached. He sat up wishing he'd said more to the kid than come back tomorrow. He wanted to know with certainty that the kid would return to their theater with his story. He wanted to wear that kid's desire for a moment or two. To feel the power in it, to taste what it was like to want something so badly. He wondered if he'd ever desired something as badly as that. Certainly he'd badly wanted to escape from his parents' farm, but that had almost happened by accident. He hadn't exactly broken free or fought his way out. He had just sort of found himself in the city one night, alone and hungry. That was six months ago. Six months! He was shocked by how long he'd been here. Shocked to think that in all that time he'd only managed to find refuge in this seedy little building.

He didn't want to face that shock, didn't want to answer the question that came with it. The question that had snuck into his life lately, nagging him in the middle of the night. Are you happier here than you were back home? Or perhaps it was the answer he was afraid to face. The same answer that always came to him: *I don't know.*

Susan

God, this bloody drumming is giving me a headache. I'm too tired and too grumpy to take on the role of saintly sister today. All I wanted to do was sleep in, but Neat had other ideas. He was standing at my doorway at ten o'clock this morning, just looking at me, saying nothing but meaning a lot. Who needs words when you've got a ten-ton mass of body language pleading your case?

"You gonna ask me politely, then?" I shouted at him.

He didn't move, so I threw back the covers and told him to get lost while I dressed.

Breakfast tasted like leather, the bus ride made me sick, and the city is too hot and too dirty today. I'm a regular ray of sunshine, I know, but I didn't get enough sleep last night. Strange dreams and faint mumblings kept me awake, not to mention the phone call in the wee hours of the morning.

It was my father, ringing from some European hotel room, his voice echoing through the answering machine speaker. "Hello? Hello?" Crystal clear, like he was in the room with me. There was a long pause, before his voice came again, distant and muffled, talking to someone in the room with him. "What time is it over there, Bel?" His pet name for my mother. It was so weird hearing him use it down the line, across a thousand kilometers of wire and satellite beams. They continued a conversation about time differences, Mother's voice fading in and out of range, Father's mumbling through the speaker, oblivious to how much this must be costing. Finally, he came to the point. "Um . . . message for Brian. How are you? Treating Verona okay?" My mother's voice interrupted him again, correcting from the background. "Verena, darling. Verona is the city." Father paused, digesting this information, then he continued. "So, just ringing to say we're fine and . . . um . . ."

Then he paused to think, the line hissing in a noisy silence. I stared at the phone, wondering if I should pick it up. Surely he wasn't expecting a conversation, he just wanted to leave a message. Then I realized, he doesn't know. What the hell was he going to do now that Neat could talk? Pack up the award? God! He was probably over there giving a talk about his book. I stood there in my pajama T-shirt at three o'clock in the morning, debating whether or not to hit him with the news. I should have told him, but he would have ruined the party by rushing home to take over. God knows I'm handling things in my own grumpy, confused way. Dad wouldn't see it that way. As far as he's concerned I'm trouble.

Susan, we have a very busy schedule over here. We don't want trouble . . .

Yeah, right. So I'm always trouble, is that it?

I didn't say that . . .

I can look after Neat. God! I'm the same age as Verena. For that matter, Neat could look after himself.

I don't think it would be a very good idea to leave him alone . . .

I didn't say that!

. . . not at this stage at least.

Father! Don't you listen to a word I say?

It's an entirely predictable conversation. Believe me, I've had a million of them before. On and on and on. Blah, blah, blah. Our scripts are well rehearsed, our roles set in concrete. The only thing that gets changed is the lines, so we won't get bored. It's safer that way, for my father and me. It means we'll never have to engage in a conversation where nasty things might be said. Where stories might be told.

Dear Daddy.

Do you remember the night you returned with your international award for *The Silent Boy* and you gave an expensive party? There were tables laden with food, drink waiters on hand, and a live music ensemble playing. I stood awkwardly in the background, dressed to perfection, waiting for my moment. And the subject of your book—not the character you'd invented but your real son—was at the tables drinking liter after liter of lemonade until I thought he would have burst open. You stood at the microphone, the glittering prize in your arms, ready to make a speech. I had something in my hands too, a homemade banner, painted in red: We Are Not Guinea Pigs.

Do you have any idea what that was about? You took Neat off his drugs a month before the book came out. You said it was because they were having a bad effect on him. But it would have been embarrassing if he'd started to speak, wouldn't it? Can't have a silent boy who isn't silent. You treated him like a guinea pig and I was going to let you know. As I unfurled my modest banner, the guinea pig materialized out of nowhere, mouth full of lemonade.

"Neat, what are you doing?" I said. "Get outa the way."

But he didn't get out of the way. Instead he leaned closer and opened his mouth, dribbling lemonade down my dress. I shrieked, I pushed at him, but he wouldn't budge. A mighty river of lemonade flowed from your son's mouth, glowing to the background music of your speech.

". . . what a great privilege it is to be among you all . . ."

"Stop it! . . ."

". . . the gratitude I feel toward my family . . ."

"God! How disgusting . . ."

Sweet, sticky river, snaking its way down my chest, splashing off my lap, forming a lake on the floor. When at last I was completely drenched, the guinea pig stopped, stepped back, and allowed me to pass. I ran to the toilet in tears, my banner awash with lemonade. By the time I returned to the party the moment had passed, the guests were all mingling, and I was so shaken it was all I could do just to stand there.

Dear Daddy, who won that time? Was it you? Or was it Neat? My silent brother who speaks volumes with lemonade.

I'm not looking forward to another dose of improvised theater. At least the drumming has stopped, but now we're into the pathetic dramas. They still haven't done Neat's. I wonder if the cute actor has been straight with us, or was he trying to be impressive? He took Neat's dream and winked at me. God! What was his name? Ted? Dan? Todd, that's it. He certainly looks like a Todd—enjoys being the center of attention, the star of the show. "Come again tomorrow, I'll help you out."

The Coat announces that they'll do the last story, raising the hat high in the air and reaching up to pull the paper out. She's halfway there when Todd bounds up with a flourish and bows to her.

"Allow me to pick the next dream, Your Majesty."

The effect is electrifying. The Coat pulls the hat out of the way, staring at Todd. He doesn't miss a beat: "The hat, Oh Great One." The Coat is blushing now, he's totally thrown her. She raises the hat high again, giving Todd a strange look. I sit forward on my seat—this is interesting. He pulls out a piece of paper, probably planted in his hand, and passes it to the Coat. She reads it, looks over at the actor, then announces Neat's dream.

"Fat boy saves world!" she shouts. The audience bursts into laughter.

I look over at Neat. His loose face is set as tight as it can possibly go, a slight twitch winking from his massive jaw. The actors huddle into a tight bunch, speaking in low voices. Then, without warning, they burst away in all directions and hell breaks loose. The musician dances around the stage area, her demonic violin screeching as the bow attacks the strings like fingernails on a blackboard. The other actors melt into the background as Todd squats in front of the stage. The musician finishes her mad dance, landing in a heap beside her drums. The hum of the city takes over.

"We live in savage times," booms Todd. "Men kill women, children watch slaughter, audiences laugh at passing bullets. We live in bleak times. Lonely wanderers lie cold and destitute on our streets, wine bottles rolling down the gutter into empty drains. We live in hollow times. Plastic objects and electronic gods are worshiped at every street corner. We are doomed!" He stands. "We are doomed!" Louder. "We are doomed!"

He raises his arms high in the air, then lowers them slowly. "Who will save us?" he whispers.

There is no answer, not a single audience member moves. I look at Neat—he is rigid, leaning toward the stage at a dangerous angle.

"You?" shouts Todd, pointing to an audience member. "Or you?"

The effect is stunning. Each person he points to

shrinks away from his glare, as if his question is an accusation.

"You!" he shouts, pointing to an elderly woman. "Will you save us?"

Suddenly a chorus of voices erupts from behind the silk screen, whispering the same phrase.

"The fat boy. We need the fat boy. The fat boy!" Their whisper builds to a demanding wail. Todd turns to the screen.

"Well, let him come then," he yells.

The screen shakes a little, the silk rustling with unseen movement. I hold my breath. How the hell are they going to depict Neat? Stuff pillows up their T-shirts? Before I can see the answer to my question, a commotion breaks out at the side of the stage. There is laughter, followed by cheering, and I look on in horror as Neat waddles onto the stage area, puffing and blowing from the exertion of getting down there so fast. Now the entire audience breaks into applause and cheering, stomping their feet at the arrival of the fat boy. Todd is thrown; he steps back a little, shooting pleading looks at his fellow actors, who have emerged from behind the silk frame. His what-the-hell-do-I-do-now? look is slowly transformed into a grin that breaks out into a huge belly laugh.

"He is here!" shouts Todd. "The fat boy!"

The audience cheers again and I groan alone.

"Tell us," booms Todd theatrically, looking toward Neat. "What is the answer? The key to this sick world we live in? Speak and we will listen."

He steps back grandly, handing the stage to Neat, and

I shrink into a ball of embarrassment and shame. I know I should stand, defend him, shout that he won't speak on demand, but I can't move.

Neat twitches a little, staring out at the audience as the seconds tick away. The moment is losing its drama, and Todd steps forward, placing an arm around Neat's mighty shoulders.

"Just one word," he says. "One word and you will save the world."

Neat looks at him, meets his eyes dead on, then turns to the audience again. There is a loud cough from behind me, followed by a few whispered "Shushes." Neat slowly raises his arms in the air, just as Todd had done, and stares at the audience. I swear some people actually move forward in their seats. I wish I could sink into mine.

"Mr. D," says Neat quietly, and he lowers his arms.

"We can't hear you," says a voice from the back.

"He said, 'Mr. D,'" yells Todd. "Mr. D is the answer to our ills."

There are a few nervous laughs, but mostly the audience is quiet, rustling uneasily. This story seems to have lost the plot, or they missed something along the way. I feel the same as they do—who the hell is Mr. D? Todd is about to continue with this farce when the Coat steps in, clapping loudly until the audience picks up that this must be the end. The Coat thanks them and gives her goodbye spiel as I quickly make my way down to the front, where Neat is standing awkwardly.

"Well, that went okay," says Todd as I arrive, a big grin on his face.

"Don't be so bloody stupid," I snap, taking Neat's hand.

I have to get out of there fast, and if it means dragging my massive brother along behind me then I will. To my surprise he comes willingly. Perhaps he's had enough of saving the world for today.

I thread my way through the crowded people traffic, offering the odd "Excuse me" whenever Neat knocks someone sideways. My head is buzzing with anger—how dare they put Neat up for ridicule like that? Allow him to "perform" in front of all those strangers, people who don't know him like I do? My anger builds, I'd like to go back and knock that slick smile off flash Todd's face. But I don't have to, a voice calls out above the din. "Wait . . ."

I ignore it at first, thinking it must be calling to someone else.

"Will you wait?"

This time I turn around to see a breathless Todd gaining on us. I want to run, get away from him as fast as I can, but Neat has stopped dead in his tracks. There's no hope of escape, now. An elephant would be easier to budge than my brother in one of these moods. Todd finally catches up with us, still wearing that ridiculous grin.

"What do you want?" I ask, sounding peeved, but, before Todd can answer, Neat grabs him in a tight bear hug that threatens to squeeze the life out of him.

Todd is a bit shocked by this affection, and probably winded too. Eventually he puts his arms around Neat and pats his back, his face buried in my brother's huge neck. They don't speak, just hug like that for ages, and I find myself feeling a little jealous. Finally, they break off and Todd turns to me, a soft look on his face. He's not so flash now, and I realize that he's really quite young, about my age. It's funny, he seemed older on the stage. I suppose they all do.

"What do you want?" I ask again, not so snappy now.

"I dunno," says Todd. "I couldn't just let him go like that. Not without saying goodbye or something."

"Looks like you've said goodbye now."

I turn to leave but he stops us again.

"Hang on, what are you so angry about?" asks Todd.

I blush instantly and say I'm not angry, but he just smiles at me.

"You think the audience were laughing at him, don't you?" he asks.

"Yes. And they were."

"No," he says passionately. "They were with him the whole way. They wanted him to save the world, really. It's just that they didn't understand what he said, that's all."

His eyes are so alive as he talks about this, so engaging, that I find myself wanting to believe him. This guy should sell cars, he'd make a fortune. I summon my most cynical sneer and say: "Yeah, right."

"Don't you believe in him?" says Todd, rocking back on his heels.

"What?" I ask, menacingly—he is on shaky ground.

"Don't you believe he wants to save the world?"

That's enough of this. Who does this guy think he is? He meets my brother twice and he reckons he knows what's going on in his head. I walk up to Todd, get as close as I can, then speak in a low tone so Neat can't hear me.

"Of course I believe he wants to save the world. Doesn't mean I'll let people like you put him up for public ridicule."

"I believe him," says Todd, staring me right back in the face.

"You've got no idea," I mutter.

"Why won't you listen to him?" says Todd. "He's saying something."

"He's saying something, is he?"

"Yes."

"Well, that's a bit of a joke, isn't it? You see, he only began talking twenty-four hours ago. After eight years of silence, he said his first words yesterday. So there hasn't been a lot to listen to, has there?"

Todd is stunned by this revelation. He breaks eye contact, and I take the opportunity to grab Neat's hand and depart. As we make our way down the street, I hear Todd's voice calling out again.

"That's even better," he yells. "It's proof that he wants to do it."

It's proof that my life is spinning out of control. I thought I was the one who knew Neat better than anybody. But it wasn't me he hugged, it wasn't me who got him to open up—it was a bunch of strangers in colored clothing, actors in a city mall. They pulled Brian out, recovered him from the pages of a best-selling book, and put him back into the world.

God, I can be bitter and twisted at times. I should be happy for Neat. I suppose I should even be thanking those people. And at least he chose me to speak to first, even if I couldn't cope with it at the time. It's funny, I always assumed that I'd be the first one he would speak to if he ever came out of his silence. And the minute he does it, I barf all over the place and go into shock.

When I was little, I used to wait patiently for him to speak again. "He's just scared," I'd say to my parents. "He'll say something when he's not scared again." But he stayed scared and my patience ran out. "It's Daddy's fault," I used to cry. "He's the one who scared Neat. He made his voice go away." Away forever, never to come back. That was what I really thought.

I slow down now, let go of Neat's meaty hand and relax. He hasn't said a word since the performance—back to his old tricks again. No way am I going to let him get away with it.

"Say something," I snap as we amble along.

He doesn't speak, of course. I think back to the last time he spoke, at the performance. What did he say when Todd asked him for the word? "Mr. D." That's bothered me ever since I heard it, it sounds so familiar.

"Who the hell is Mr. D?" I ask.

He doesn't answer.

"Come on, Neat!" I yell. "Why do you just talk for them? What about me? I'm your bloody sister."

"Mr. D," says Neat softly.

"Yeah, I heard that one already. Who is he when he's at home?"

"Our friend."

"Our friend. What, you mean yours and mine?"

He nods.

Mr. D. I've never heard of him, have I? Maybe it's a code, or a nickname for someone we know. It wouldn't be Father or Mother, Peter and Belinda Bennett, no Ds there. I'm not a D, Verena wasn't a D. God, I'm desperate now—who else would Neat know? Then it hits me, or rather creeps up on me from my memory. An outing with Father, a guilt-induced trip to the Agricultural Show. One of the rare moments when we almost seemed like a family—proud father and two lovely children. Except one of us was bloated and strange. We were at the shooting gallery, the sideshow blaze of lights and sounds so alien to my father's world. He probably looked upon it as research, getting among the masses. But he was enjoying it—I can see his smile. He paid for some pellets and shot at a few ducks. He missed every time. In the end the guy at the shooting gallery felt sorry for him and gave him a prize. A yellow, fuzzy blob—it's slowly taking shape—a treasured object that Neat loved with all his heart. We used to play with it together, include it in our spy games.

Mr. D, the fluffy yellow duck, our friend.

Todd

He was hooked by a crushing bear hug in the middle of the city, by a jacket of flesh that nearly pulverized his bones. The fat boy wanted him in his story, to be part of that amazing desire that burned in his eyes. And Todd wanted it too, but it wasn't going to be easy, especially with the sister hovering around like a guardian angel.

There was something that was both fierce and enticing about her—frightening too.

What an amazing pair of characters they were. Todd couldn't get over the way the fat kid had waddled onto the stage. Arriving all sweaty and puffing, yet totally focused and present in his role. It was like standing next to lightning. And Todd had been hit, struck down by the fat boy's dream. Like most victims of lightning strike, he wandered around in a daze. Then he realized that he had no way of contacting them again—no address, no phone number—he didn't even know their names. His daze turned into despair. Unless they came back to the theater, they were gone forever, lost in the city. Todd kicked himself for being so stupid. What was he going to do now?

When he arrived back at the amphitheater he was set upon by a grim-faced Carrie. How dare he take over the show like that? How dare he alter the format of her theater? And how the hell did he know the Bennett boy anyway?

The Bennett boy? Todd couldn't believe his ears as Carrie told him how she'd recognized Neat as Brian Bennett, the subject of the book *The Silent Boy*. The fat boy has a name, the angel has an address, they are real! Todd grabbed Carrie by her face and kissed her.

"What are you doing?" she shrieked, but all Todd could do was kiss her again and shout, "Thank you, thank you." Tomorrow he would begin his search.

The next morning he went to the library to borrow a copy of *The Silent Boy*. He told himself he would have to do a bit of research first, find a way in. But mostly his "research" covered a growing feeling of uncertainty. These were real people he was dealing with here. It had been easy to treat them as characters he could manipulate in his fantasies when they were anonymous. Now that he knew they were a famous pair of kids, he was a bit scared.

It took him a while to locate the book—he was a total novice when it came to libraries. He sat down at a table and turned the volume over in his hands. Here, laid out in hundreds of pages, was the life of Brian Bennett. A photograph of Peter Bennett, Susan's father, was inside the cover. He looked like a kind man, trustworthy, with Susan's and Brian's eyes.

Todd turned to the first page and read.

I had a son once who spoke with the music of childhood. Those bold boasts and daring challenges and heartfelt emotions of growing up. He cried, he sang and he laughed. He queried every detail of life. Then one day his music began to fade away, so slowly it was almost gone before we noticed. Now all that is left is silence. Uninterrupted, immovable, a wall of nothing.

The music is gone.

I have a son who is a silent boy.

The words conjured up an image of a frail, beautiful boy lost in a romantic world of silence. It was a bit hard to match with the waddling, sweaty kid who had stumbled onto the amphitheater stage yesterday. Todd flicked through the pages of the book, the words flying past his eyes in a blur. He came to a set of photographs in the middle. Here was a very young Brian, his sister next to him, smiling at the camera. She was six and Brian was ten. They looked like ordinary kids. There was nothing of the magnetic gaze of the Brian Bennett that Todd knew.

He wondered if, after years of silence, of wrapping yourself in your own world, it was natural to come out with an intense desire like saving the world. Todd touched the shiny pages of the photographs, these flat, black-and-white kids who had entered his life. And now he wanted to enter theirs, step in and answer the call of the giant hug. Respond to the message of a fat boy's powerful drama.

He took the book home and lay on his bed trying to read, but his attention kept wandering from the page. How would he get into the life of this fat kid and his sister? The idea of actually becoming involved was scary. It was easier to sit back and let things happen, like an audience member. Like the way he treated the freak show here in the boardinghouse—as a casual observer, waiting to be entertained. But he couldn't do that with the fat boy. It would go against the very grain of his nature to step back when everything told him to jump in. He itched. That was how he thought of it. His whole being itched to get in there and become involved. He had to go for it, not to be entertained or to stop the itch, but to satisfy an almost primitive urge to act.

The next day he caught the bus to the tidy end of town and walked along winding streets with magnificent views, to be finally confronted by the Bennett house. It was something straight out of the movies.

No wonder they weren't hiding the address, thought Todd. You couldn't miss this place. The house was all windows and columns and an immaculate lawn that was large enough for a cricket match. Todd wanted to turn back, so alien and daunting was this world. Instead, he took a few deep breaths and gave himself a pep talk. Deal with the fact they were rich. Deal with their fame. Then deal with the sister who looked like she could eat him for breakfast.

He set off up the drive with a hopeless feeling. Halfway along the drive he noticed something glinting in the bushes and quickly stooped to grab it.

Arriving at the Bennett front door he pressed the doorbell, expecting it might play a few bars of Bach, or perhaps roar like a lion. A very ordinary ding-dong rang through the house. The sister took her time to answer, only coming after Todd had pressed the button for the third time. When she opened the door and saw him, a curious mixture of humor and anger swept over her face.

"You don't give up, do you?" she said eventually.

She hadn't slammed the door, she hadn't threatened to call the police. The game was on. Todd grinned, then shot a quick question at her. "Have you asked him who Mr. D is yet?"

"No . . ."

"Bull. You have, haven't you?"

"How did you find this place?" asked Susan, trying to change the subject.

"Did you ask him?"

"What the hell if I did? It's got nothing to do with you. So why don't you go away?"

Now she went to close the door, but Todd held up the shiny object he'd found in the bushes. It was the silver candlestick that Neat had shoved into Verena's mouth during her grand exit.

"Here," said Todd, waving the candlestick in the air. "I brought you this, as a sort of peace offering."

A glimmer of laughter crossed her face, softening her eyes, and Todd felt slightly encouraged.

"Cost me a whole week's pay," he continued, placing the candlestick in her hand. "But it was worth it."

Now she laughed, and Todd cast his eyes down, the trickster taking over momentarily, the clown's modest smile, the elaborate bow.

"You're full of it," she said, putting the candlestick on the foyer table.

"Okay, so I found it in your bushes. It's still a peace offering. Can I come in? Is your brother home? And who, or what, is Mr. D?"

Todd walked into the foyer without waiting for an answer, pushing the game further. He tried not to let his eyes pop out at the obvious signs of wealth that surrounded him.

"Nice little flat you've got here," he said slowly.

"We like to think of it as home," said Susan.

"Have you lived here all your life?"

"Yes. Well, until I was sentenced to hard labor at an expensive boarding school."

"Ooh. So you're a bad girl, really?"

"I try my best," she said. "How about you? A model of saintly purpose, I suppose. Mother's angel, the creative member of the family?"

Todd turned his head away and pretended to look at a painting on the wall. "No," he said quietly, "they call me the idiot." He looked up at her now and grinned, an outrageous memory lifting his spirits. "I hitched out of town last year on my seventeenth birthday; haven't been back since."

She seemed to be impressed by this, and he took it as enough encouragement to walk down the hall, looking for the kitchen. He just had to keep moving, doing something, making himself part of the atmosphere until she accepted that he wasn't going to leave. He found the kitchen and opened the fridge, aware of how outrageous his actions were. Something told him she liked it. He pulled out a carton of milk, grabbed a glass from the sink and poured himself a drink. Then he sat at the table.

Susan sat down at the opposite end of the table. It was such a curious mixture, her face. Soft lines that could so easily transform into harsh angles. Quick, sparkly eyes that could so easily shoot lethal darts. Her fluffy, closely cropped hair that could so easily look tough and mean. She smiled now, slowly and deliberately.

"He's a duck," she said.

"What?" asked Todd, looking at her carefully. She wanted to play, had a mischievous look. That was a good sign—he was in for the moment.

"Mr. D," said Susan, looking satisfied with the impact

of her statement. "You wanted to know who he was. Well, Mr. D is a fluffy yellow duck that my father won at the show when we were little kids. Not quite as mysterious as you hoped, is it?"

Todd held Susan with a straight, poker-player's face, pausing for seconds that threatened to turn into minutes. Eventually he asked, "Why a duck?"

"I don't know . . ."

"No, it's a line out of a Marx Brothers movie: 'Why a duck?' "

Susan stared at him, anger flashing in her eyes, those angel eyes. "Well, that's useful to know."

"Sorry." Todd shrugged. "It just popped into my head."

"Thanks for the help, I feel a hell of a lot better now," she snapped. "You want to know something? At least when Neat was silent I could pretend that there was something going on in his brain, some sort of deep-down thought process. But now he's talking, it's brought out the truth. There's nothing deep there at all, just a fluffy duck we used to play with as kids. So just at the moment, I don't need you quoting the Marx Brothers at me."

He blushed deep red. That had been a stupid thing to say. Up to now he'd been trying to act interesting, funny even, but all he'd done was piss her off. But she was still with him, she hadn't retreated, yet. He took a breath.

"You're wrong," he said quietly, meeting her eyes and her anger.

"What?" she yelled.

"He's not crazy, if that's what you think. He really wants to save the world and I want to help him if I can."

"Hello," said Susan, knocking at an imaginary door. "Mind if I interrupt with a reality break here? He can't save the world, in case you hadn't noticed."

"Sure, he can't do much for all the crap in the world, but he can do a lot for hope . . . if that's something you still believe in."

"Gee, how inspiring," snapped Susan. "Is that a line out of one of your plays?"

"No!" yelled Todd, banging the table with his fist.

Susan jumped with fright, and Todd apologized, embarrassed by his outburst. He hadn't meant to lose his temper, but her cynicism had slipped under his guard. Just like the daily sneers his family dealt him, the relentless attacks on his sanity, his sincerity. He was sure his outburst would have lost her, but she was smiling now.

"You didn't like that, did you?" she said.

"No," said Todd slowly, uncertain of her mood. "I didn't like it. But I could say the same to you. What's so real about what you say? Where is the real Susan Bennett? Certainly not the person who is sitting here right now."

"No?" Susan laughed. "Well, who am I then?"

"You're a mask."

"A what?"

"A mask. An attitude that covers the real you," explained Todd. "Just like I'm a mask. Right now I'm probably wearing my 'nice-guy' mask, desperately trying to convince you that I'm sincere . . ."

"Well, you're failing," interrupted Susan.

He ignored her comment, staring at her blankly. It was an exercise they played during rehearsals, holding a look at the audience without covering themselves in a "mask" of any emotion. He held the pause for a long time, and Susan started to squirm in her chair. To confront someone whose face was totally neutral was very unnerving. Todd knew that he was taking a risk, but he had a point to make.

"Stop it!" she shouted.

"You didn't like that . . . did you?"

"Ooh," said Susan, mocking him, "a little bit of payback, was it?"

"No." Todd blushed. "I wanted to show you something. It's an exercise I've done in drama . . ."

"Oh please . . ."

"It feels uncomfortable to be stared at like that . . ."

"Yes, because it's rude . . ."

"No!" said Todd. "You were afraid that if I looked long enough, I'd see the real you. I'd be the same—everyone is. But not him, not your brother. He doesn't wear any mask."

"He doesn't need one, he's got his yellow duck."

"He's not going to stop, you know. Until something happens, he'll tell you, me, anyone he meets he wants to save the world." *Just like I did*, thought Todd. *Just like I kept acting, giving voice to the real me, throwing myself onto any stage I could find, until I found one where I was accepted.* But it had cost him his family life, his country-town home, his security, just to pursue his dream. What was the cost to the fat boy?

"If we don't listen to him," said Todd carefully, "if you ignore him or I ignore him, then what's his next choice? He might stop again."

"Stop speaking?"

"Yes. Only forever."

She glared at him, a hint of terror in her eyes, then stood up and walked out of the room.

"Well," said Todd to himself. "That seemed to go pretty well, didn't it?"

He shuffled in his chair like a schoolboy. He'd been locked out of the plot by this walking contradiction, this wild-eyed, soft-skinned, shaved-head terror. One of his mother's phrases came to him: Susan Bennett had him "walkin' dizzy and talkin' silly." Todd gave a twisted smile which turned into a grimace when he remembered how he'd told her the story of hitchhiking out of town on his birthday. He couldn't imagine what had possessed him to tell her that and to make it sound so cool. Looking back, it hadn't been cool. It was miserable, desperate, and in the end lucky.

He remembered coming home that day, his birthday, walking into the kitchen, squinting from the sun that pushed through the grimy window; seeing the cake spoiling on the table, bathed in afternoon light, half-burned candles and dusty streamers nearby, waiting to be decorations. He knew his sister had done the baking, following the recipe on the back of a packet. She would have retrieved the streamers out of the bottom drawer as well. He probably should have been grateful that someone had bothered to make an effort, but instead he felt angry.

The dusty, pathetic decorations totally summed up his parents' attitude to him. He was the outsider, the nuisance, the extra mouth to feed when times were tough. He didn't fit in. Those neglected birthday treats just twisted that sick, hungry feeling in his guts to the point where he had to walk out. Down the drive and onto the highway, a long walk by city standards, head low and guts easing, arms out wide, trying to catch the wind. He just wanted to fly, float away on a breeze that took him as far from home as possible. He might have looked like a strange bird, or a free spirit, out there on the road, but to the driver of a semi he looked like a hitchhiker. When the huge rig pulled over, Todd ran to the passenger door as it was swung open by the driver. "You hopping in or what, mate?"

Todd just stood there, blinking, taking in the possibilities. Before him the highway, stretching all the way to the city, to another world; behind him a tasteless birthday cake in an empty kitchen. So he climbed in, possessing nothing more than the clothes he stood up in and an overwhelming urge to get into that truck and go.

"I'm Todd," he said, shaking hands with the driver.

Seven hours later he was in the city. The only person he knew was a woman who had come through town with her drama production earlier in the year. The actors ran workshops at the school, and she'd pulled Todd aside and told him he had exceptional qualities, that he should think about a career in acting. But what the hell was her name? Todd wandered the streets trying to remember it, finally coming up with the name of the theater company. He looked it up in a torn phone book and rang the number, his first conversation in the city with an answering machine. Next day he tried again, grimy from his night under a tree, relieved when a voice answered and knew who he was talking about. He caught the bus out to the theater, slept that night on the stage and was in their production by the end of the week. He believed in fate, believed that he was meant to coincide with that semi driver. He also believed there were times in life when you act first and think later. His mother was always accusing him of rushing in like a "blue-arsed fool." And, like a blue-arsed fool, he climbed those steps into the truck's cabin. The road would always lead him in the right direction.

"Even if it is to the Bennetts' kitchen," muttered Todd, looking around at the shining chrome and polished glass of his surroundings. There was no sign of Susan. He shrugged and stood to leave when she returned, plonked a dirty yellow duck onto the table before him and said, "Ta da!" Todd smiled at the fluffy little peace offering, knowing he was still in with a chance.

"I'd like you to meet the savior of the world," said Susan with a satisfied smile. "I don't know about you, but I feel a hell of a lot better just knowing that Mr. D is here to protect us. You feel saved yet?"

"No," said Todd.

"What?" said Susan in mock surprise. "But this is the duck, without a mask, without artifice, a saint in yellow fluff. Aren't you going to convince me that this duck is genuine? That he is the only truthful duck in the world?"

"I couldn't convince you of anything if I tried." Todd laughed, feeling a weight lift from his frame. "So why should I try?"

To his amazement, a look of disappointment crossed her face, and her body language said "defeat." He couldn't work her out at all—what did she want from him? She must enjoy the sparring, the push-shove-backtrack, taking the smacks on the face, giving it back in spades.

"I'm not a fighter like you," said Todd.

"Me!"

"Look, I'm here because your brother came to me, and I haven't been able to get his story out of my head."

"Why?"

"I don't know." Todd shrugged.

"You're a hope junkie," said Susan.

"Am I? I thought I was just kind, warm, and open."

"You junkies are all the same—full of denial."

"And what am I supposed to be hooked on? This?" asked Todd, holding up Mr. D.

She shook her head and sighed, saying in a barely audible voice, "I don't know."

Todd was shocked by her mood change. He felt her sadness. What a time she must be going through, this confused sister who loves her big brother. Watching him suddenly talk, expecting he might say "hello" or "I'm thirsty," but instead he says he wants to save the world. Up to now, he hadn't thought of her as part of the plot. She was the obstacle, the annoyance he had to get around to help her brother. But her sudden return with the duck had changed his perspective, like a mood shift in a performance. He was compelled to respond to that change, to shift from the sparky energy he fed off during their front-door encounter. To respond to an ache he felt in his own heart for this girl who didn't know where to place herself in this massive story her brother had invented. Todd spoke gently.

"He came to me, Susan. Came to my theater because he had something to say. I don't think he's said it yet."

He could see that she was listening, and he knew he had to continue, but he had no idea what to say next. A wild idea sprang into his head, and he grabbed hold of it desperately. "What if . . ." he said, and stopped.

"What?" she asked.

"It's pretty stupid . . ."

"Tell me," said Susan, cautious but interested.

Todd stood up and started pacing the room, feeling the need to move. A rush of ideas buzzed through his head. "Okay, he wants to reach out to the world—that's why he came to our theater."

"Sure," said Susan, "that's obvious."

"So, theater is limited. But there is another place you could go to that would really spread your message about saving the world."

"Which is . . . ?"

"TV," said Todd, smiling. "We get Neat on TV."

"Oh," she said, slumping back into her chair as if to say, "I thought you might have had a real idea." She sighed and looked out the kitchen window. "No TV station in their right mind is going to put my brother on their show."

"Ah," said Todd, playing his last card with a flourish, "you're forgetting about community TV."

"Why would that be different?"

"Have you ever watched community TV? It's amateur time. I mean, I had this friend who did work experience at the community TV station and on his first day they all went home and left him in charge. He could have put anything on the air."

"How would you do it?" she asked cautiously.

"They have a show called *Voice of the People*. He could go on that. Everyone gets one minute."

Todd knew that Neat could do it. He'd stood up on the stage in front of those strangers and spoken. What he'd said hadn't been too deep, but there must be something more there. You don't break an eight-year silence with the news that you want to save the world unless there's some substance behind it. Everything was up to Susan now—whether or not she believed Neat could do it. She seemed lost in thought, and Todd wondered where she had retreated to. What lay behind that far-off gaze, those sad eyes? He felt his breath rise and fall with hers, his muscles tighten, his body poised. He was in her hands now. He would wait for her reply. If she said yes then he would go on. If she said no then he would not. It was exciting to be held that way, to be a mere part of a twisting, turning plot.

The pause was long, and Todd wondered if Susan was doing it deliberately, paying him back for the stare-you-in-the-eye trick he'd pulled on her. He was about to speak, move her to answer or just break the silence, when a deep voice did it for him.

"Mr. D wants to go on TV," it said, and for a moment Todd thought that the duck had spoken. But it was Neat, waddling into the kitchen in his pajamas, stretched to their button-holding limit.

"Mr. D and me," said Neat.

"What is this?" said Susan, staring at Todd. "Why does he always talk to you and not me?"

"I don't know." Todd shrugged. "Ask him."

Neat had reached Todd's chair by now, and was bending over, as much as he could bend over, hugging the actor by the chest and neck.

"I think this means he wants to try out my plan." Todd grinned.

Through the encroaching flesh, the mountain of body that engulfed him, Todd could see a half smile appear on Susan's face. Then he remembered—she hadn't answered him. He felt disturbed by that. Where did her heart lie? Yes or no? He wanted to search her face for meaning, but he was too busy coping with the fat boy. His body struggling with the bulk of Neat's hug, his heart struggling with the weight of her ambiguous smile.

Susan

Bus travel with my big brother is always an interesting experience. He likes to perch in the middle of the back-seat, like a sort of a grand toad or beanbag, watching over the aisle with an impassive stare. It's the only place large enough to accommodate his enormous bum and he becomes anxious if it's not vacant. That usually leaves the rest of the backseat for me to shimmy into, nodding with embarrassed smiles at the other commuters. But this city-bound trip is a little different, because I have Todd to share my seat with. If we had any sense we'd sit on either side of Neat to give ourselves some room, but somehow we chose to squeeze together. The chubby messiah and his two disciples, off to the promised land of TV to deliver the message.

I wonder if anyone has actually told Neat yet what the message is. I certainly don't know, and I can guarantee Todd is making it up as he goes along. He'd call that improvising. I call it guessing. Todd says he believes in Neat—I suppose that's the sort of thing you do with messiahs. And where do I fit in? I'm the smiling donkey in the corner of the manger, looking on as the two boys hug each other.

There was a kind of poetry in their embrace. I guess I was expecting Todd to be clever or theatrical, the way he was at my front door. Instead he was honest, vulnerable even. That little-boy question in his eyes. I wonder what answer he was expecting from me?

He's squashed up against boy-mountain right now; I'm by the window, Todd's leg warm against mine. Did he deliberately put it there, or was it an accident? I don't cope all that well with physical touch. If I pull my leg away now, will he think I put mine there just to touch his?

I don't usually trust theater types. My only exposure has been the drama queens back in boarding-school hell, and those gals hunted in packs. Todd's not like them, maybe because he comes from the country. He's sort of soft, and the way he looks at you, it's like he's giving you something. He has an open face, deep blue eyes and dark hair that add up to a very cute effect. And I bet he doesn't even know it. He told me a bit more about himself, how he came to the city alone from his parents' farm. I couldn't imagine doing that. It's so brave and decisive. Besides, where would I go? Not back to boarding school. Maybe I could run to his parents' farm. What would it be like there? His parents sound like tough people, but maybe they're honest too. There's not a lot of honesty where I come from. Just half-truths and evasive silences and little colored lies.

"So," I say to Todd in a cheery voice, "you always follow people around after you've done their stories?"

He smiles, a mischievous look sparkles in his eyes. "Of course." He grins. "That's how I get my buzz. I'm a very empty person who lives life through others . . ."

"I knew it. I could tell by the shifty look in your eyes."

"Actually," he says, serious now, "I do love hearing other people's stories."

"I don't," I say. I'm trying to sound too interesting. Have to back off a bit. But it's okay, he's smiling at me, even nodding.

"Most people don't," he says. "It can be very boring. But it's different in the theater . . . the whole setup. The ritual of the stage and the audience, it kind of takes it out of the ordinary into something sacred . . ."

"Sacred!" I laugh. "Get real. A bunch of wankers telling stories about wanting to drive a bigger car is not sacred."

"Not those stories," protests Todd, "the special ones. Like Neat's. I dunno, maybe sacred's not the right word . . . but the unexpected stories . . . they do lift everything. Well, anyway, I like it."

"I'll tell you why you like it," I say, on a roll now. "You're a voyeur—you like watching people from a safe distance."

"No, that might be you, but it's not me. When I try on their stories, I have to get into their lives completely. If I did that from a distance then the performance would be piss-weak. You've seen it, you know how powerful it can be."

I remember my story, the assassination of the famous man, how it made my skin crawl at the time. Todd turns his body around to face me, the pressure on my leg a little stronger. He's almost bouncing on his seat now with excitement. It's not cool, it's not sophisticated, and I like it.

"Okay, your turn now. I'll tell you what you're into."

"Oh yes, what?" I blush.

"You're a word person."

"No," I say, shaking my head. "I don't trust words."

"You do." He laughs. "You love words. Look at the way you use them."

What? Like my father? Is that what he means? It's funny—if anyone else had said that, I would have gone for the jugular. Do I love words? Those harmless little ink blobs that can spin a web of deceit, that can pierce your heart with a callous disregard? Maybe I shouldn't blame words. After all, they're just the building blocks of lies and truth. Father believes he searches for truth when he writes with words, even when he invents it. I invent everything when I use words, even when I long for the truth.

"Okay," I say, not wanting to bring the conversation

down with my father-crap. "So I'm the word person. I write the plays, you act in them."

"Have you written a play?" He's like an eager puppy.

"No." I laugh. "I wrote some stories once . . . won the national Bookmaze Young Writers Award."

"Really? That's pretty impressive."

"You'd better believe it. I plagiarized the lot. Stole them from magazines and obscure novels, changed the characters a bit and called them my own."

He stares at me in disbelief and I shake him, feeling playful.

"Hey," I say. "It takes a lot of talent to plagiarize properly. The newspapers came around to take a photo of me with my father. You know: daughter of famous author wins literary prize."

"And what happened?"

"I threw up all over the carpet."

"No kidding."

"Happens all the time."

"I'd like to read them," he says.

"You wouldn't."

I'm enjoying this game. I can say things to him, push him around a bit. He doesn't back off, he sticks around.

"Tell me a story then," he says, "if I can't read one you wrote."

"What? So you'll act it out here on the bus?"

"I'll try to restrain myself." He smiles.

"You'd better, or I'll kill you," I say, sounding a bit too much like I mean it. I start to talk fast so he won't think I'm some sort of demented bitch. The words start spilling out of my head. "I was sent to boarding school because I was a bad girl. I know you find that hard to believe, but I was. My mission in life was to give my father hell, and I did."

"What did you do?" he asks.

"You don't want to know about it . . ."

"I do," he says.

"Um . . . once Dad was going to do an interview with an overseas magazine. Real big-time stuff. They'd faxed him the questions, crap like 'What inspires you?' So my father had these questions on his desk, and I got hold of them and sort of . . . well, I answered them. Faxed my version of his inspiration back to the magazine."

"You're kidding," he says, eyes popping.

I wish I was kidding, but it is the total truth. At the time I wanted to hurt my father as much as I could, and destroying his international reputation seemed like a good place to start.

"What did you write?" asks Todd.

"Nothing . . . It was a long time ago . . . it's dumb."

"Oh, come on. Don't stop there." He looks disappointed.

"You're so funny." I laugh. "Okay. Um, they asked him if he considered truth to be a casualty of modern times. Very heavy, intense stuff. So I wrote back that 'as an author, I consider the truth to be mine to do whatever I want with.' I think I added, 'Never let the truth get in the way of a good story.'"

"Bloody hell." Todd laughs. "Did they find out?"

"Yeah, well, the magazine rang him and wanted to verify some of the answers. I mean, here was a world-famous author of a so-called true account of his silent son virtually admitting to lying."

"Wow. Remind me never to get you angry," says Todd. "Your old man must have really been awful."

Well, it's hard to say who is the more awful in all this—me or dear Papa. It'd probably be a dead heat. The long war between my father and me is definitely not one of Todd's sacred stories. More your dirty, bitter, bleeding-knuckles type of story that goes on and on and on. I opt for a more sanitized version today; no point in scaring the lad to death.

"My father responded to my little 'prank' by sending me to boarding school," I continue. "At the tender age of fourteen."

Fourteen! That was meant to sound dramatic. It doesn't. It just sounds miserable.

"It was like, 'Bye-bye, Susan, do try to come back normal.' And you know what? I nearly did." I laugh. "It was such a relief to get away from all that crap at home . . . I was a refugee. God, boarding school seemed like heaven for a while there. I threw myself into it totally—the model student. I breathed in their garbage and spewed it out at all the right moments."

As I speak, as the words spill from my mouth, I have this weird feeling that I'm both the teller and the listener. It all sounds familiar, yet I'm hearing it for the first time. I watch every flicker on Todd's face, I scan his eyes, ready to pounce on any signs of retreat. You wanted to hear this, buster, so you'd better stick around. But he isn't retreating, he's right in there, listening. I don't think I've ever experienced this before, to have someone so open and ready to hear what I've got to say.

"So what happened then?" he asks.

"Along came the drama group. They were putting on a play about Joan of Arc. One of my roommates was in it, and all she could talk about was what an incredible woman St. Joan was. She'd huddle under the blankets at night, learning her lines by torchlight, sighing deeply. Here she was, the queen of modern appliances, worshiper of small plastic cards, telling me about the life of someone as up-front as St. Joan. She didn't even have a fraction of St. Joan's courage and vision, none of the girls in that school did. Sure, they could talk about admiring St. Joan, or women like that, but what had they actually done in their lives that actually meant anything? That was when it hit me. What had I done? I was no different from them. That had probably been my parents' plan all along. I was a do-nothing queen heading for a do-nothing life. Congratulations, Susan, you've finally joined the family."

I stop for a second, catching my breath, letting it sink in.

"That night I borrowed a razor and shaved my head. I just did it, like I had this clear choice to make. You should have seen the reaction from the goggle-eyed little beauties the next day. They thought I'd turned into the bitch from hell, and they were right. The bitch from hell was a far better persona than little Miss Gray Blob. At least I was making a statement . . . well, I thought I was. They kicked me out after that."

Todd just looks at me, and I swear if he's doing that neutral-face, stare-you-in-the-eye trick again I'll bust his nose. But I don't get a chance to work out his reaction because the bus jerks to a halt and Todd quickly nudges Neat in the ribs.

"This is our stop."

We follow Neat down the aisle, waiting patiently as he negotiates the steps. I feel a bit foolish now. Todd probably thinks I was trying to impress him with my story. Hell, I didn't even know half of that stuff was going to come out. We finally make it off the bus and are given a foul-mouthed farewell by the driver before he shuts the door behind us and speeds off down the road.

Todd turns to me, squinting in the harsh afternoon sun, and says: "So you both found a voice."

"What?" I sound a bit snappy because I'm still not sure if I'll have to bust his nose open.

"You and Neat, sounds like you found your voices at the same time. You were in sync with each other."

I look at him, a bit stunned. I hadn't thought of it that way. He doesn't wait for a comment from me, just leads off down the street.

And the vocal Bennetts follow.

Todd

The COMM TV building was a low, cream brick box with a badly painted sign tacked to the front. Glass doors led into a grubby foyer that smelled of stale cigarette smoke and plastic. An old wooden desk and a tattered partition were the only furniture—both desperately trying to look official. The effect was spoiled by the graffiti carved on the desktop. Over by the wall was a trash can stuffed full with empty pizza boxes and surrounded by an army of beer cans. Todd called out a few times, but there was no reply.

"Looks like the lunatics have fled the asylum," said Susan. "We could go in and take over. Broadcast subversive material."

Todd smiled, enjoying her sparky humor. She was a natural with the words, a storyteller, a sharp thinker. He liked that, liked listening, liked watching too, her eyes so warm when she relaxed, her smile expansive. Sitting on the bus, he'd found himself studying her fine-boned features, his fingertips tingling at the idea of touching her skin, perhaps accidentally, just to see if it was as smooth as it looked. Pressed up against her leg, he'd had the sense that they occupied the same place. Not on the backseat of the bus, but somehow in the whirl of the city, in the press of people, they were breathing the same kind of air. The feeling was impossible to describe completely, and he knew that she would probably scoff at him if he tried, but it was enough for him to know it was there. Enough also to know that she was there, and to feel the quiet tingle on his fingertips. To know that her presence made easy breathing difficult during mundane tasks like traveling on a bus or standing in the foyer of a run-down building.

The sound of a toilet flushing heralded the arrival of an extremely thin, thirty-year-old man wearing tight jeans and sporting a greasy ponytail.

"Yeah, can I help you?" he said, tucking his shirt into his jeans.

"Um, yes," answered Todd. "We want to get our friend here onto *Voice of the People*."

The man shook his head and muttered that they weren't taping that show today.

"Come on," said Todd, "it's very important."

"Yeah, it always is, bud."

A girl in her mid-twenties with dyed black hair and several nose rings poked her head around the partition, which was concealing a narrow corridor.

"What's up?" she asked.

"It's okay, I'm handling it," said the man, a bit short and tetchy. The girl vanished. Susan moved closer to the ponytail man and touched him on the arm. He wheeled around and stared at her hand, as though she might be sprouting talons.

"Hey," she said. "Have a look at my brother."

He turned to regard Neat through bloodshot eyes, and a look of amazement crossed his face.

"He's big," he whispered.

"He's more than big," Susan whispered back. "He's Brian Bennett, Peter Bennett's son."

"So what?"

"Have you heard of the book *The Silent Boy*?"

"Might have."

"That's him. He's famous and he wants to speak for the very first time on your TV show."

"Yeah?" said the man, scratching his stubbly cheek. "Tell me more."

Susan gave a brief sketch of Neat's last few days, his emergence from silence with a mission to save the world. Interest grew on the ponytail man's face as he was drawn into the story. Eventually he put his hand up and said, "Okay, you got me." Then he yelled: "Tess, fire up the Sony, we've got a little taping to do."

Susan

The sound of raised voices echoes through the building as we stumble into the studio, which is nothing more than a small room with a few lights strung across the ceiling on metal poles. There is a camera on a tripod nearby, pointing toward a stool. The stool has been placed before a large sheet of blue paper.

"Looks like this is the spot," says Todd.

The shouting continues. Obviously the girl, Tess, she of the nose rings, is not happy about our intrusion. Ponytail enters, looking a little flustered, and tells us everything is cool. Somehow I don't believe him. He tells Neat to sit on the stool, but the tiny thing creaks ominously. A unanimous decision is then made that Neat should stand, which he does. Ponytail fiddles around with the camera, probably trying to fit my brother in.

"Have you gone over what Neat's going to say yet?" I ask Todd.

"I tried to on the bus, but he wasn't listening," he replies.

I walk over to my big brother, who is the picture of awkwardness, the fluffy duck clutched to his stomach.

"This is it, Neat," I say. "Your chance to tell the world what you want to say."

"Mr. D," says Neat.

"You're going to have to say a bit more than that. No one knows who Mr. D is."

He looks at me, nodding at this bit of information.

"Okay," says Neat.

"I hope so," I mutter under my breath as I take up a position behind the camera. Ponytail is happy now and calls out the studio door.

"You there, Tess?" There is no answer. "Could you please press Record?" Still no answer, so he runs out and does the deed himself, dashing back in breathlessly. This guy obviously needs to take on a better fitness regime.

"Okay," says Ponytail, "let's go."

Neat shrugs his shoulders and starts to walk out of the studio.

"Where's he going?" asks Ponytail.

"You said 'let's go,'" explains Todd.

"Is he retarded or something?"

"No, he is not retarded," I say through clenched teeth. "Just talk to him."

"Um, Brian," says Ponytail, "stand back where you were . . . yes, that's it. Now, when I say 'go,' you stay there and start talking."

"When you say 'go' I stay," Neat repeats.

"Yes, and start talking."

"Now?"

"Just a minute," says Ponytail, looking through the viewfinder. "Okay, go."

My whole body jumps at the word "go." What the hell is he going to say? Part of me wants Neat to do the predictable thing—stand there in silence. That's how it should be, how it has always been. It's familiar and I know I can cope with it. But another part of me has wild expectations. Neat will blossom from this moment, find voice for his strange desire to save the world, have something significant to say. In fact, have anything to say at all. That would be miraculous enough, a sort of saving of the world in itself.

My roly-poly savior shuffles from one foot to the other, looks down at Mr. D for some kind of inspiration, then shuffles a bit more. Finally he looks up and asks: "Can you see Mr. D?"

"If you mean the duck, then yes, I can," says Ponytail.

Neat nods, smiles at his duck, then shuffles again.

"I think this is going to be embarrassing," I whisper to Todd.

"Give him time," he replies.

I don't know how much more time we have. Ponytail is starting to look agitated, standing up from the camera and giving Neat a get-on-with-it look. Miss Nose Ring pokes her head into the studio and says, "Can I have a word with you, Phil?"

Phil of the ponytail looks a little perplexed, then points to the camera. "Look, it's still recording, okay? I'll be back in a minute."

He exits and I see Neat relax a little. I find myself relaxing too. The voices resume their concerto in the background and I say softly to my brother, "It's okay. You can say whatever you like. Whatever Mr. D thinks you should say."

Suddenly Neat looks inspired and stops his shuffling. He looks at the duck, and I know this sounds bizarre, but I swear he's having some kind of conversation with it. This goes on for about a minute, then Neat looks up and addresses the camera.

"I don't know if I have much to say," he mumbles. A pause. Is that it? Is it over now? Then Neat continues. "But I want to . . . I want to save the world. So does Mr. D. Because . . . I know how bad . . . um . . . sad it can get. I've been sad . . . buried in sadness for a long time. And I've been quiet about it because that made me strong. Never said a word to no one, not until Mr. D told me I could speak and still be strong. I know I can save the world, I know I can. I know you can be strong too. You can do whatever you want to . . . Mr. D knows that . . . I know that. I did. I came up again. You can too. That's all I have to say. Sorry if I wasted your time."

And so it is done—my big brother bear has spoken his piece. Tears well up in my eyes, and I take a step closer to him, moved by his eloquence. I want to hug him; I used to hug him all the time when I was little. Until now I've been afraid to touch him, afraid that he will reject me. His eyes make contact with mine, a slightly dazed look on his face. I reach out, but a loud voice cracks the moment.

"Great speech!" It's Todd. He places his arm around my shoulder in a friendly hug and babbles on about what Neat said. My whole body is jangled by his voice, like it's giving me electric shocks. I desperately want to get away but I'm too stiff with my own embarrassment. These drama types, they're all the same, everything's feely, touchy, huggy, wonderful. I finally disengage from his embrace and gush something stupid about how Neat always had it in him. All the while my face is burning hot and my guts feel sick. God, don't throw up, not here. Neat waddles out with his hand between his legs, looks like his speech has moved him to the toilet. I'm about to follow when Todd bails me up again.

"That bit about buried in sadness," says Todd. "God, how moving. It's like he was giving us the key, you know, to why he stopped talking. Do you ever wonder about that?"

"Not really," I mumble, just wanting to get out fast.

"Doesn't it interest you?"

"What?"

"Why Neat stopped talking? He might be revealing something. I feel so privileged just to have been here to hear it."

"Privileged?" I say, trying to stop my head from spinning out. What is he talking about now? Can't we just get out of here? This place is so stuffy.

"The whole world has read that book, you know, and here is Neat talking about what happened from his side . . . I dunno . . . for the first time."

Is that it? Is that the little gem of information he wants from me? That sordid little piece of Bennett history? And what will he do with it? File it away in his collection of "sacred" moments? I've got to get out of here.

"I'll see where Neat is," I gasp, staggering out of the studio.

I wander aimlessly through the rooms, just trying to get my head back together. How dare he want to know about why Neat stopped talking? Who does he think he is? Has he been asking Neat questions? What has my brother told him? Why does he want to know? What's it got to do with him, anyway? What's anything got to do with him?

God! Listen to me. I sound like a paranoid bitch. Todd probably doesn't know anything, he's just being eager and curious. Innocently stumbling into the cesspit of Bennett secrets—into me. A shaven-haired warrior-woman, cut off from the comfort of human touch. My skin is so dry and brittle. That's why I needed to hold my brother. There was so much at stake back in that studio, so much in my little step toward Neat, my pathetic attempt to reach out to him. I can take rejection from just about anyone, except Neat.

My wandering takes me around in circles, until I come to a room that's different from the others. It is darker and larger, and I burst into it like a diver surfacing for air. I just want to stop this madness. There is a big TV set in the middle, showing the output of COMM TV, and from the corner of the room I hear sighing followed by quiet voices. Two bodies embrace in the corner of the room, love's triumph for all to see. Phil found Tess, or maybe Tess finally found Phil. Their bodies so close, so intimate, so exclusive. A great wave of sadness comes over me. I feel numb, my head coming to a dead stop.

Stumbling out of the room, I make my way to the front door where Neat and Todd are waiting. As I approach, Todd turns to face me and I freeze. In that moment I realize with absolute certainty that I'm afraid of Todd's eyes. Afraid that they might find their way into the truth of me. Past my defenses to the very heart of me. The warrior-woman rises up. She's a fierce fighter ready to protect me from the dangers of eye contact. For a moment I debate whether to unleash her, whether to wreak havoc on the innocent. Just for a moment—then I decide to do the decent thing. I go blank. At least that way no one's going to get hurt.

Todd

Dirty brown rivulets of water leaked from the shower onto Todd's head, failing to wake him up. He felt as piss-weak as this shower. It was nearly twenty-four hours since he'd been dismissed by Susan outside COMM TV. She'd come out of the building with a dead look on her face, as if her soul had vanished, leaving nothing but an empty outer shell.

"So listen, thanks for what you did," she said, staring distractedly at the traffic.

"Yeah, no worries," Todd replied.

Then she started to walk away. Todd couldn't move. Outrage and panic had transfixed him. Surely she would snap out of this daze and turn to him, invite him to a coffee shop so they could debrief. It wasn't until she'd nearly vanished around a corner, with her bulky brother in tow, that he realized she wasn't coming back.

How dare she treat me like this? he thought. He might have stood there all day if that tiny spark of resistance hadn't given him an idea. With desperate pace he ran after her, catching up at an intersection. She turned to him, her face a path he couldn't navigate.

"Here," he said, scrawling his address on the back of a bus ticket. "In case Neat wants to contact me."

She took it without comment and was gone.

Todd hated himself for using Neat as his excuse. It was Susan Bennett whom he wanted to see again. Working with her had been cool, making Neat's TV appearance happen. He didn't want it to stop . . . at least, not like that. But all he could say was "Bye."

Todd turned off the taps slowly, then started drying himself in front of the clear mirror—no steam, not enough heat. He moved his face close to the glass, his breath fogging the reflection. The more he stared, the more unreal it looked—the shapes, the contours, the fine hairs and tiny freckles. He fell into that unreal space, merged with the blurred shapes and the shades of skin tone. There were no clues in the shapes, no answers as to why Susan had cut him out like that. Just the colored blobs of an abstract painting.

The bathroom door clicked, and Todd turned around wildly to see the old woman from number five standing there. She had a half-smile on her face, and Todd quickly wrapped himself in the towel.

"You finished yet?" she asked.

"No," said Todd incredulously.

The woman stood her ground, as if she was going to wait at the doorway, watching him finish his bathroom business. For a moment Todd was stunned, then he turned back to the mirror and made a great show of squeezing pimples on his forehead. The sound of her fluffy slippers shuffling back down the hallway brought relief. There was something creepy about the way she'd stood there and simply accepted his naked presence in the bathroom. The lonely kid from room number three.

Todd walked noiselessly down to his room, dressed quickly, then paced, feeling the need to kick a hole in something. The events from yesterday played over and over in his head. How had he offended Susan? Was it when he talked about why Neat was silent? Was that it? But surely that couldn't be such a sensitive topic? After all, it was in her father's book for everyone to read.

He grabbed the paperback and lay on the bed, flicking through the pages, trying to find a passage that explained Neat's silence. The photograph of Susan's father stared up at him from the inside cover. This was the man who was supposed to be a tyrant, if you could believe anything Susan said. The man she'd been at war with for half her life.

After a few minutes of flicking, Todd chanced upon a section about theories. It was full of medical-sounding phrases. He tried to concentrate on words like "elective muteness," which was some kind of childhood condition, and "malingering," which meant Neat was doing it deliberately, but his attention kept wandering. The most he got out of it was that Susan's father wasn't keen on these theories.

How can you box a person with descriptions? The human condition is so flexible, so massive in its scope that all the theories of medical science cannot explain what really goes on in a person's head—my son's head. He chose silence: that is the only and inevitable conclusion I can come to. He chose to be in his world. To watch. To think. To hide?

Todd closed the book. He was beginning to wonder if anyone knew why Neat had stopped talking. It seemed a bit of a cop-out to say that he chose to be silent, and just leave it at that. Why didn't Peter Bennett have any theories of his own? Parents have always got something to say about what their kids are up to. Like his own parents, with their monosyllables and their haven't-got-time attitude—even they would have a fair idea why he'd chosen to run away. He tossed the book to the floor; it offered him nothing.

The muffled sound of the moaner from room one crept into Todd's room. Why couldn't he keep his fantasies to himself?

Todd stormed out into the hallway, banged his fist on the moaner's door and shouted, "Shut up!" Then he flung the front door open and escaped.

Out on the streets he took to prowling, hoping to be distracted by the bustle of the city, to pluck life from the passing breath of strangers. But the footpaths were just dirty today, the people ugly, the walking tiring, the air smelly. No entertainment here, no weird characters to turn him on. No fat boys and bald sisters to gobble him up and spit him out.

Todd leaned against a factory wall, the late afternoon shadows deep across the road. Was this it, then? Was this the end of his desire? Was this where the skinny kid from the country belonged? He'd escaped from high school drama nights where he played with all his heart, while his parents squirmed uncomfortably in their seats. He'd come from suffocation to gulp down the adventures of the streets. Was this the air he'd sought to breathe? Was this the "home" he'd dreamed of? A place that didn't give a rat's arse if he was alive or dead?

The sound of shouting distracted him, and he looked down a laneway to see a man in a business suit standing in the middle, feet spread wide and arms flailing. There was blood on his face.

"Come back, you little pricks," he shouted.

The blood had spoiled his clean white shirt. On the ground lay his open briefcase, the contents scattered about, fine sprays of red over the pages. Todd took a few steps toward him to see if he could help, but the businessman wheeled around and shouted.

"What the hell do you want? Eh? You want a bit too? Little bastards. Come on, pal, I'll splatter your face across the wall."

Todd froze, a slow panic rising from his chest and up to his face. He could feel his cheek twitching as the man snarled at him.

"Sorry," said Todd croakily. "Sorry." Then he turned and ran.

It was almost dark by the time he arrived back at the boardinghouse. He pushed the front door open, switched on the hallway light and nearly fell over with shock to see Susan and Neat waiting there for him. They looked uncomfortable and a bit lost. Todd swore under his breath.

"Sorry," he said, fumbling for his key. "I was out."

"Neat wanted to come," said Susan. "To see what you thought of it."

Todd stared at her, wondering what she meant. Then

it hit him like a kick in the stomach. Neat's TV appearance—it had been on today.

"I didn't see it," he mumbled, finally getting his door open. "Actually, I don't have a TV."

He ushered them in, embarrassed by the dim little room. If Susan was appalled by the conditions, she was doing a good job of not showing it. She perched herself on the edge of his bed, the only place to sit in the entire room. Neat sat down next to her, and the bed frame groaned. Todd sat on the floor, his back up against the smudged yellow wall.

"So what was it like?" he asked, trying to sound chirpier than he felt.

"Good," said Susan. "You okay?"

"Fine," he lied.

"Why didn't you tell us you don't have a TV?"

"I didn't think of it." He shrugged.

There was an awkward silence.

"Look, maybe we shouldn't have come," said Susan.

"No, stay," said Todd, a little too forcefully. "I want you to stay. Sorry, I'm in a bit of a crap mood. This place is really giving me the shits. So, tell me about it, what did he look like?"

"Well, he looked like Neat, but skinnier."

"The magic of TV." Todd smiled.

"Mr. D was on TV," said Neat.

Before Todd had a chance to ask what he thought of the show, Neat stood up and walked out of the room.

"So this is home, eh?" said Susan, ignoring Neat's departure.

Todd stood and switched on the light, loosening his shoulders a little. Then he sat at the other end of the bed and kicked his shoes off. "Sorry if they smell," he said, "but I've been walking for hours."

"Yeah, I think I'd go for walks too if I lived here."

Todd stared miserably at the tea-chest "table" next to his bed, the clothes stuffed into plastic bags, the bare window that looked out onto a brick wall.

"You were in a weird mood at the TV station," he said eventually.

"I'd just had a shock." She told him the story about the two lovers, and, even though Todd laughed, he could sense she wasn't being totally straight with him.

"He was so old," Susan shuddered.

"That's nothing; you should see the couple in room five." Todd laughed.

"I don't want to know."

He lay back against the end of his bed and grinned at her, relaxing again. The barrier had gone, replaced by a sparkle, and he felt his mood lifting with her presence. The Susan from the bus ride was back, that ready-to-play look in her eye. He told himself that she wanted to be with him too, that he could see the evidence in her eyes.

"So, how's Neat?" he asked. "Does he still want to save the world?"

"Who knows?" Susan shrugged. "All he said after the TV show was, 'I want to see Todd.' Didn't say anything about whether the world was saved now or not. Anyway, as far as I'm concerned, Neat's world-saving days are over."

"What do you mean?"

"I mean I've had enough."

"But what about Neat?" said Todd. "What about what he wants? He's not retarded or anything. I mean, you yourself said that. Isn't it up to him?"

She glared at him, sending a crystal-clear message that he'd stepped into dangerous territory. Sometimes it was like walking through a minefield, trying to talk to this girl. What was he allowed to talk about? Certainly not her brother. She was the only person in the world who could have an opinion on him.

Susan bent down and picked up the copy of *The Silent Boy* from Todd's floor.

"What the hell are you doing with this?" she asked.

"Reading it. Or at least, trying to."

"Why?"

"I just . . . I wanted to know more about Neat, I suppose . . ."

"Wasn't the real thing good enough for you? Anyway, it's all lies, so you're wasting your time."

She was so agitated, screwing the book into a tight roll in her hand. Todd cursed himself for leaving it lying around. Of course she'd see it the wrong way; it didn't take much for her to do that. He wanted to say something to make her stay, but he was sure he'd only make it worse. Everything seemed to slide into disaster with her, as though she couldn't have a good time for too long. Susan held the book up, her face twisted with some kind of powerful emotion: half misery, half pain.

"Everyone wants to use Neat. My father used him to

write this. Doctors and speech therapists tried to use him to become famous. I'm the only one who really knows him. I'm his sister, so ask me, not this piece of crap." She threw the book across the room.

"I'm sorry," said Todd, not knowing what else to say.

She cut him off, shaking her head, saying, "I'd better go now." There it was again, the wall, the barrier that put him at arm's length.

"Don't," said Todd, standing now. "Please . . . I couldn't bear it."

"Couldn't bear what?" she said haughtily.

"The big cut-off number. Like what you did at the TV studio yesterday . . ."

"I don't know what you're talking about."

"I'd like to be your friend, really. But it's like . . . you won't let me or something."

"I wouldn't bother," she said, closing her eyes. "I'm not worth it."

"Yes, you are," said Todd, but his words sounded pathetic. He wanted to break down her barrier and drag the real Susan out from the rubble. Instead he said "sorry" again, wincing as the word came out.

"I knew it was dumb to come," she said, turning toward the door.

"Susan . . ." He was interrupted by shouting. It came from the hallway.

"Where's Neat?" yelled Susan, sounding a little panicked. She ran out the door and Todd followed. Mr. Pritchard, Todd's landlord, stood alone in the hall, staring into room one.

"Who's that in there with Mr. Goodman?" he asked.

"What's the matter?" asked Todd.

"No one goes into Mr. Goodman's room—he specifically asked me," said the landlord.

Todd peered into the darkness, the moaner's lair.

"Is Neat in there?" asked Susan.

Todd couldn't see, so he took a step in, and was instantly hit by a foul smell—a mixture of putrid clothing, rotting vegetable matter, body odor, and stale air. Todd gagged and placed his hand over his nose and mouth, adjusting his eyes to the gloom. A dark burlap curtain was draped over the only window, a useless covering considering the layer of grime that was caked on the glass. A black-and-white TV set cast an eerie gray light over a bare, stained mattress, where Neat was squatting, clutching a pile of old rags and burlap. At least it looked like rags to Todd, until he noticed hair and arms and legs and feet. Neat was speaking to the bundle, gently, as if he were addressing a two-year-old. "I saved you," he said, over and over.

It was the moaner in Neat's arms, a putrid, revolting old man, yet the fat boy cradled him like a precious object. The fat boy's hands held him tenderly, supporting brittle bones as if they might snap in the wind. Todd turned away quickly to see Susan at the door, trying to get in. She was blocked by the landlord, who was bent over, dry retching. She pushed past him, also retching at the sight before her.

"What's going on?" she shrieked.

Todd shook his head, unable to put the scene before him into words. Susan bent over her brother, holding out her hand.

"Come on, Neat. Let's go," she said.

He ignored her, continuing to rock the old man like a mother putting a child to sleep.

"Please," begged Susan. "Let's get out of here."

But Neat was immovable, a solid mountain of flesh, a huge hamburger of comfort and warmth, holding the old man.

"Oh God," said Susan, looking around, wild panic in her eyes. "It's disgusting."

"Susan," said Todd, but she ignored him, repeating her summary of the situation over and over, like a chant.

"Susan," said Todd again, softly. Then louder, "Susan!"

She turned to look at him, her breath coming in short, hard rasps. "You did this. You and your stupid idea. You told him this was possible. Look at him, clutching some disgusting retard!"

"Hold on," said Todd, trying to sound reasonable.

"It's your fault," she raged. "This isn't a game, you idiot! Look at it. It's disgusting. Oh God!"

Todd closed his eyes, unable to cope with her fury.

"Open your eyes!"

He felt a sharp slap across his face. Susan let out a loud, ascending cry that froze him to the spot. She slapped his face again. "You did this." She repeated the accusation over and over, slapping wildly like a child. All Todd could do was put his arms up to protect his face. With each slap he felt her fear cut through his skin, slice through his protection, planting the seed of shame. "You did this!" and he believed her. His bright idea had exploded in his face.

She stopped suddenly, stared wildly at the room, as if seeing it for the first time, then walked calmly out the

door. Todd sat heavily on the floor, the muted sobbing
of the "moaner" playing in the background.

Neat

In the dark room he feels at home. Feels like he knows
what lives here, why it lives here, how it lives here. In the
dark end of the world, where a small shuffle can be
the highlight of the day. Where all else fades away, into
the dark, dark room.

His eyes register it all before they can actually see, before they take in light, they know what to find. His body
knows too. As soon as he opens the door, his body
knows. The tingling of his skin, the flaring of his nos-
trils, the tightening of his rectum.

The rags and filth are just different versions of his own
story. Here it is, here is his past, his beginning, his history.
Here's the perfect place to start. He goes to the man,
sprawled upon his throne of rags. The dweller in the dark
props up on one elbow and croaks in a voice that has lost
the memory of conversation. "I saw you—on TV?"

"I am Neat," he replies. "I've come to save the world."

"Thank God," says the old man. "Thank God. I
thought you'd never come." The rags fold in on themselves as the dweller in the dark collapses into tears.

"With my arms," whispers Neat. "I'll take you there
with my arms."

A powerful liberation overcomes the fat boy. He feels
the past explode from his skin like a discarded shell, and
he almost floats with the sense of release it gives him.

The way forward is clear. He can see it like others see the sunshine. His eyes pierce the grimy walls that surround him, looking far into his future.

His future, the fat boy's. The time has come to digest the world that surrounds him. Eater of pain, of sorrow, of mangled hope, that is what he will be.

He looks down at the rotting bundle in his arms and swallows the stench of failure as if it were an insignificant bubble.

2

THE YES
GAME

Tribune Press

17 February

Odd Spot

HERE'S a story more bizarre than fiction. Ex-TV-quiz-show-host Lucky Goodman was found locked away in a shabby boarding-house room by Brian Bennett, son of world-famous author Peter Bennett. Brian Bennett is the subject of his father's prize-winning book, *The Silent Boy*. According to witnesses at the scene, there is nothing silent about Brian now. He appears to have found his voice again, loud enough to start on Comm TV's "Voice of the People" this week. At the time of his "rescue," Lucky Goodman had occupied the front room of the boardinghouse in a state of abject squalor for the past three years. He was reported to be dazed and confused, and is now in a stable condition at Memorial Hospital, recovering from malnutrition.

Tribune Press

1 April

Odd Spot

We have before us a media release befitting April Fool's Day (although we think it is for real). Community TV station COMM TV has announced a new show, entitled "Fat Boy Saves World," starring Lucky Goodman and Brian Bennett. "Who?" you might ask. Regular readers of this column will know that Bennett, the so-called mute, subject of his father's internationally famous book *The Silent Boy*, rescued Goodman from a life of squalor six weeks ago. Goodman was Mr. Quiz Night in the late seventies and eighties, one of the highest paid celebrities on television. Gambling debts followed by mental illness saw him slide into obscurity, until he met Bennett. The show will "provide quiz questions, laughter, tears and a bit of homespun philosophy from Brian and Lucky, who have been to the bottom and returned safely." Personally, I can't wait. This has all the hallmarks of a cult classic. You can catch "Fat Boy Saves World" on Saturday afternoons at 5:30 to find out if the world gets saved.

Susan

If hell is where bad girls go and heaven is for good boys, then all the freaks, creeps and losers must end up here, in the foyer of COMM TV. At least that's the conclusion I've come to. I base my judgment on the assorted ferals crowded into this filthy place, no doubt escaping a windy Saturday afternoon. Or perhaps they have come to witness the birth of my brother's television event. I think *Fat Boy Saves World* could quite possibly be the worst TV show ever made. Perhaps that's why I'm here. Just like a passing spectator at a road smash, I'm both horrified and attracted by the sight of blood.

There is a girl at a desk who is in charge of the foyer. She seems to be in a poopy mood. Must be Nose Ring's sister. I suppose I'll have to announce to her that I have Brian Bennett and his newfound friend, Lucky Goodman, the stars of COMM TV's newest show. Neat won't tell her, he's too busy mumbling in Lucky's ear. The girl raises her eyebrows ever so slightly as we approach.

"Yes?" sighs Little Miss Poopy Mood.

"We're here for the . . . ah . . . my brother's show."

"What show is that?"

At this precise moment our relationship turns ugly. If she thinks I'm actually going to say the absurd title of this even more absurd TV show out loud, then she's either on drugs or traveling with the fairies.

"Tell her the name of the show, Neat." I nudge my big brother, but his co-star chips in instead.

"What is the papyrus plant used for?" Lucky Goodman asks in a deadpan voice. "What are the colors of the Swedish flag?"

Now I want to die. For the past few weeks I have had to suffer this garbage bin of droning quiz questions, walking around half-dazed in my father's ill-fitting clothes. I doubt if he even knows what planet he's on. But the minute he thinks anybody is talking to him, out comes a question. He's got a million of them stored in that fried organ masquerading as his brain.

The girl with attitude stares at Lucky like she wants to rip his tonsils out. It's a feasible suggestion. "Wait over there with the others," she orders eventually, indicating the loose assembly of misfits in the foyer behind me. Neat and Mr. Goodman amble off to the toilet. I shrug at Miss Poopy Mood and wander casually into the fray.

I inherited Lucky Goodman a few weeks ago, when an ambulance arrived at our house and deposited him at the front gate. Someone had put our address on his hospital form. "What the hell is this?" I yelled. "Circus time?" I tried arguing with the ambulance drivers, but it was a lost cause. These guys would have dropped him off at the zoo if it meant getting away from those quiz questions.

"What is the capital of Ecuador? What is the single largest crop to come out of the USA? How many times will twenty-two go into 484?"

"You sure this is where you live, mate?"

"Who was Romeo's father?"

"We'll take that as a 'yes,' then."

I suppose it was inevitable that Lucky would end up with my brother. He's been slowly dying, wasting away in his dim little room. Then one day he sees an enormous boy on his TV who offers a mumbled promise of salvation and Lucky waits. Along comes the fat boy, and their bizarre relationship begins. God, I still get goose bumps when I think about that day. How it changed everything. But I don't dwell on it for too long. I can't. It was just an aberration, that's what I tell myself. A passing hiccup on the breath of my miserable life.

What a pair these two crazy bookends make. They've been in that toilet for a few minutes now, but I know exactly what they're doing. They have their heads together, locked in a long, whispered conversation that no one else can hear. It totally freaks me out when they do that, furtive little grips on each other's shoulders, mumbling like monks, faces so serious. But then, I've never been any good in the company of whisperers. And I cope even worse with questioners.

Questions are a pain in the arse. If I had my way I'd declare them illegal. Perhaps not Lucky Goodman's questions—they don't mean anything. They don't challenge me to dig down into the cesspit I laughingly call my emotional state. I mean the ones that come from the eyes of young boys with cute looks. The ones that threaten to touch me deeper than I care to be touched. It was too many questions that released the warrior-woman that afternoon in the boardinghouse. I wanted to tear Todd apart with my will. Hell, he had it coming, didn't he? I mean, why couldn't he hear my warnings? Why did he have to keep at me when I wanted him to back off? He's well and truly backed off now, anyway.

See how successful I am with boys?

The stupid thing is, I feel really bloody sad that Todd has gone. Shit! I'm a mess. There's tears in my eyes. Here, in the foyer of this stupid TV building. All because of a nosy actor who happened to be standing in the way when I lost it. "I'm trying to be your friend." That's what he said to me, and I slapped his face off. Well, he'll just have to deal with it like I'm dealing with it.

Shit! I wish I *was* dealing with it.

At least I managed to get Neat home. I found him at the hospital—he'd gone there with Lucky Goodman. Then I locked myself into my room and cried for four days. But you know what I really wanted to do? Scream like a kid in the middle of a tantrum. I couldn't do it. Yep, I'm coping fine, thank you very much.

The assembled weirdos in the foyer are coping too. There's a large girl in the corner reading a book, her lips going a hundred words to the minute, quietly mumbling the same phrases from the same page that she reads over and over again. It's either a very complex piece of writing or no one's taught her how to turn a page yet. There's a skinny-looking kid with an electric guitar; he's trying on the ice-cool approach. I can't be bothered telling him that his fly has broken. There's an old couple who look like they'll cry if anyone talks to them, and there's a shaven-headed tough guy who keeps giving me the eye, like I might be part of the same secret bald society that he belongs to. Maybe it's time I let my hair grow again.

If this audience is anything to go on, *Fat Boy Saves World* looks set to create television magic. It's all Ponytail Phil's idea, he's the brains behind the "concept." Phil baby turned up not long after Goodman to convince Neat that his "special brand of audience appeal would make great TV." What a total load of crap! Ponytail was just trying to cash in on a little fame, make a name for himself. The newspaper article about Neat finding Lucky Goodman was the first bit of true publicity he'd ever earned. Phil wanted more, and he was practically salivating about it. "It's like a character from a book has come to life," he said. I was just about to slam the door in his skinny little face after that remark when Neat invited him in. I protested, but they ignored me.

I suppose you could say my official role as the sister-nanny ended right there. As far as I'm concerned, Neat's on his own from here on. Let him be used up by Phil, the spin doctor of community TV. "Neat's future is up to Neat." Todd had so succinctly reminded me of that.

I could have killed the whole deal if I'd wanted to. The perfect opportunity actually presented itself to me one dreary afternoon. I was walking past the telephone when I noticed that the light on the answering machine was having a fit. I'd turned the machine on to cut out the world. Who the hell had been calling? Todd?

It turned out to be worse in a way. Father and Mother, taking it in turns to call from overseas. Why wasn't anyone answering their calls? What was going on? They left a number to call back on. It would have been so easy to pick up the phone and tell my father about the talking, tell Mum about the TV show. Then sit back and watch it hit the fan. But I couldn't do it. Maybe because I'm so used to lying to my parents, or because I'm so used to protecting Neat. Whatever, I put them off. Phoned them when I knew they'd be asleep. My father woke to my bright, jolly voice.

"Everything's fine . . . just having trouble with the phone . . . what am I doing home? Holidays, Dad . . . (they never were any good with dates). Yes, yes, Verena is coping well . . . she's learning English . . . Well, she doesn't have to be here all day . . . Neat's fine, really . . . everything's fine, just enjoy your trip . . ."

It was pretty unconvincing stuff, and Dad sounded a bit suspicious. I'm usually a much better liar. I hung up the phone feeling sick, stranded in the middle of nowhere, belonging to no one.

The two mumblers finally emerge from the toilet and separate, moving among the crowd like a couple of old pros. Neat barely speaks to me these days—my one strong anchor point in the world hardly notices I'm there. He's too busy mumbling with the Quiz Show King of 1972, the man with a million questions and no answers. I guess I don't fit into the equation. Now Neat goes over to the girl with the book and stands next to her, looking straight ahead, no attempt at conversation. Goodman approaches the timid couple in the corner, spewing quiz questions at them. Finally the Ponytail emerges and I almost feel glad to see him.

"What are you two doing out here?" asks Phil, looking more than a little flustered. "We go to air in half an hour."

He ushers Neat and Lucky past the uninterested girl at the desk. I give her a significant smile as I pass and she gives me the two-finger salute.

The set for *Fat Boy Saves World* is something to behold. Shaggy old couches have been arranged against the bare brick wall of the studio. Someone has tacked old posters and pictures onto the wall in a hopeless attempt at "brightening" it up a little. A vase of tired flowers sits on a small coffee table, and two glasses of water keep it company. The scene is bathed in an orange-yellow haze, courtesy of the studio lights overhead—all five of them. No expense has been spared for this bold new concept in programming.

Couches are moved to the left, then back again. People wander onto the set, then off again. The camera nearly falls off the tripod, and Phil is stamping his foot for quiet. The odd assortment of weirdos from the foyer shuffle in—they're the "live" audience, although some of them look half dead. Finally a hush comes over the studio, somebody calls out "ten seconds," and a girl wearing headphones gives Phil a big wave with her arm. He rushes into the middle of the set with a microphone in his hand.

"Good afternoon and welcome to *Fat Boy Saves World*," he yells. "Coming to you live from COMM TV, UHF 32 on your dial."

I can't watch, I feel so embarrassed. Neat's going to make a fool of himself, I know it. I close my eyes and pretend to be somewhere else. Phil is droning on in the background, giving a potted history of the fictional Brian Bennett. "Silent for eight years . . . the subject of his father's famous book . . . until one day he woke up and decided it was time to speak, time to save the world." It is such a mush of meaningless words that after a few minutes it melts into the background, becomes verbal wallpaper. Then a now-familiar voice leaps out of the "wallpaper," and I look up.

"Hello," says Neat. He's holding the duck to his ear, like it's whispering to him. "Mr. D wants to say hello too. I listen to every word he says, but don't worry, he's just a yellow duck."

Ah, that voice—what trouble it has caused me these past few weeks! What power it holds over me! So deep and rich and exclusive, saved for strangers on TV shows. It used to be mine, once, when I was little. It used to be my evening prayer, my nighttime guide, the soundtrack to my dreams. Now Neat speaks for the world he wants to save, the world of faceless strangers who are desperate enough to watch community TV on a Saturday afternoon. The world of whisperers, mumblers and outcasts who have bounced and ricocheted off the sharp edges of society, only to land here in a grungy TV studio. They are Neat's people, I'm not.

Now I realize just how lonely I am.

Todd

He sat nervously in the old theater's foyer and waited. His name would be called soon, he would have to perform, to drag the clown out of himself. If Todd had been less terrified he might have seen the events that led him to this place as a kind of theatrical journey. He might have even wondered where the journey started. With the letter? Or did it begin earlier than that? Was it the madness in the moaner's room that began his journey?

Todd left the boardinghouse that night dazed, sleeping out in the open, promising himself he would never have to return. It was a promise he kept for a week or two, camping out on sofas and floors, courtesy of his Theater of Possibility friends. Sharp images stabbed at his sleep: the terror in Susan's eyes, the pathetic bundle of rags in Neat's arms, the landlord vomiting in the corner. Dark wraiths that he'd conjured from the sorcerer's pot by daring to enter into the lives of the Bennett children. He'd encouraged the fat boy to believe in a dream that had turned into a nightmare.

That's what he believed, until he read a newspaper article about *Fat Boy Saves World*. Neat had kept the dream going. Todd thought about the last time he'd seen the fat boy —when he was cradling the sick Mr. Goodman. Neat wasn't giving up or going under, he was right there in the present, holding on to the world he wanted to save. Todd began to see that the nightmare had been his own, not Neat's. His own deeply felt failure, brought on by the slaps of Susan Bennett. He had been totally out of his depth with her, with the awesome power of her emotion.

He tried swimming out of that power—laughing with Dave from the Theater of Possibility about this crazy girl who went completely mental on him. Said he was glad he wasn't tangled up with her anymore. But in his nighttime dreams he drowned in self-pity—where had he gone wrong? He still felt hurt.

Then he broke a promise and returned to the boardinghouse to collect his things. He could have sent a friend, but there was something he had to face. A memory of her—soft, angry, laughing. A memory of terror that still panicked him, still made his hands shake. But when he opened the dirty front door, the image wasn't there. All he could see in the dim corridor was the bathroom lock, where it lay like a victim of some violent crime. Todd entered his bedroom, trying to be very brisk and businesslike about gathering his stuff. That was when he found the letter.

For a brief moment he thought it might have been from his family, until he realized they didn't have his address. He ripped open the envelope and read that it was an invitation to audition for a drama school he'd applied to months ago. He stood there, stunned, unable to decide what it was that life had thrown at him this time. Dirt or stardust, disaster or opportunity? He didn't need to look at Mr. Goodman's door on his way out to be reminded about life. You either jumped in or watched.

The audition gave him a focus, an opportunity to forget about the past weeks. He even felt normal, devising an audition piece around the character of Arlechino. He recognized a kindred spirit in Arlecchino, the cheeky, scheming, thieving character from the Italian commedia dell'arte theater. Todd borrowed an Arlecchino mask from his theater friend, Natalie. Standing in her lounge room, he put it up to his eyes, covering the top half of his face with a colorful, leathery leer. It left his mouth and chin free to add to the spirit of the mask. He slipped the elastic over his head, then turned to Natalie and grinned. She squealed with shock; the lifeless mask now had life, soul, character. Todd was possessed.

He worked at Arlecchino every day, tickling away at his own sadness, playing little tricks on life so that it belly-laughed and burped and dropped its purse of gold. He rediscovered his own trickster—the bowing fool at the Bennett doorstep, the artful player on the amphitheater stage—and started to feel alive again.

That was when he declared war on the miserable, thin mattresses on his friends' lounge-room floors. He went out and found another place to live, a little cottage next to a spray-painting factory that he could share with two engineering students. As soon as he moved in he began to sleep better, despite the fruity smell of paint fumes, and dreamed often about the farm and his little room out the back that caught the morning sun and the magpies' call.

His mind started to burn with ideas, and he kept an exercise book where he wrote down plots and sketches and character notes. He told himself he was emerging from the past, so it was curious that he chose that moment to contact the past. He tore a sheet of paper out of his exercise book one afternoon, put his address on the top and wrote a quick letter to his parents. It was a spontaneous urge to contact them again, to fill out his life for them. With this letter they could picture him in his house, working at the theater, prowling the city streets. When he'd finished writing he read it through before picking up the pen again and scribbling wildly onto a new piece of paper. This time his writing was rambling, incoherent, confused and circular. It was a letter to Susan Bennett. The words stumbled onto the page, crashing into each other as he tried to grapple with what he wanted to say. It was pure emotion he sought to put on that page, too messy for mere paper and ink, and he ended up throwing it away.

And so he came to the audition and his terrified wait in the theater foyer. His one glimmer of hope for the day had been to read another newspaper article about Neat. The first episode of *Fat Boy Saves World* would be taped that afternoon. Todd had sent a silent wish of hope to Brian Bennett.

Fifteen eager hopefuls sat around in the waiting area, straining to hear what the poor sap on the stage next door was doing as an audition piece. Is it better than mine? Have they used my ideas? Do I have a chance?

"You're next," a woman with a clipboard and a frozen smile whispered to Todd as he sat on the edge of his chair. He nodded and went over the piece he'd prepared. He would walk onto the stage as himself, remove the Arlecchino mask from his bag in absolute silence and play a game with the audience. Tease them until they were desperate for him to place the mask over his face and become Arlecchino.

"Todd Parson" came the call, and he took his last calm breath.

The hollow sound of the wooden boards resonated in his ears as he walked onto the stage, glimpsing the judges in the muddy theater light. He took up his position and adopted a shy little-boy face. Teasing the audience, he held out the bag, peeking inside a few times before slowly opening it. He shared a "what could be in here?" look with the audience, then reached in carefully and removed the mask. Placing the bag on the floor, he took hold of the elastic around the mask, ready to place it over his head. The elastic should have been tight, but it hung loosely from the leather. What the hell did he do now? If he stopped to explain about the mask, or walked off to have it fixed, the whole buildup would be ruined. His game with the bag, his look of wonder—all lost. He would never get this harsh audience back on his side again. He was stuffed.

Then he paused, barely breathing, and found a tough knot of resistance in his heart. Not yet, he thought. Not now or ever. He wasn't ready to go down without a fight. He hadn't walked out of his parents' kitchen that day to give up over a lousy piece of elastic. Gripping the mask tightly, he nodded his head slightly and leaped into the unknown.

He quickly turned his back on the judges, hiding the mask from their view. The elastic could be threaded back, with time, and Todd's fingers worked fast. He maintained his character, turning to the judges and giving them a "don't-you-peek" look. A smile from out of the gloom lifted his spirits. Working quickly at the elastic, he gave the judges another glance, tutting "uh, uh, ah." Finally the mask was fixed and he placed it over his face, noticing the transition in his body to Arlecchino. Suddenly he felt grounded, like he belonged right there on the stage. Arlechino the cunning fool, Arlecchino the trickster, recognized the importance of the situation and bowed low to the critical audience. "You oh-so-gracious judges, your majesties, your holier than holy holinesses." At the bottom of his sweep, arms swinging behind him, Todd the actor, mere vessel for the universal fool, emitted a loud fart. The judges erupted into laughter. From somewhere behind the mask, Todd knew he was on his way.

This was what he loved about acting, the wild spontaneous moments that can make or break you, the quick chance decisions that lead on to the wonder.

The yes game.

The woman with the clipboard told him after the performance that they'd be in touch and thanked him for his time. Todd walked home feeling exhilarated, that one moment of laughter playing over and over in his mind. He'd done it, he'd faced down the demons and proved his stuff. This was a fantastic day. This was a day to celebrate.

Neat

"I am the eater."

This is what he has come to realize since that day in Mr. Goodman's room. Why did it take him so long to know that?

All those years hiding from noise. All those years watching the pain through a transparent wall, and all he had to do was eat it. He is a great pit of empty hunger that will eat and eat and eat until all the pain and misery and smallness has gone.

His new friends think they are hiding their secret hurts from him, but he sees them. Swirling stories that spin and scribble across their features. So big and obvious and tasty, they are nothing more to him than a plate full of hot dogs. Down they go. One by one by one. Now he can see his friends without the distraction of those scribbles, see their pure faces in the light, and he knows exactly how strong they can become.

Like this girl here on the couch. Oh, she could be so strong. Mr. D sees that too. Mr. D, a fluffy yellow duck. Even he has stories swirling across his features. But they are someone else's pain, someone else's bad memories from so long ago. The fat boy doesn't like to look at them for too long. There is nothing tasty about these stories, and he knows that for the moment he will not contemplate eating them.

He will contemplate the new instead, like the girl on the couch.

"Rosie, hello."

Susan

Neat is sitting on the couch next to the girl with the moving lips, the camera close and wobbly, almost up their noses. She looks absolutely terrified. Could this be a chat show section of *Fat Boy?* Just the two of them, nattering away about the latest movies they've seen, Hollywood gossip, a few tips on fashion followed by a favorite recipe? I doubt it. The chubby Messiah stares at the girl like one of those phony hypnotists.

"Rosie, hello," says Neat. She doesn't make a sound. "Mr. D wants to know what you're reading."

Rosie's eyeballs nearly pop out of her head as she glares at the book, the one page that she reads over and over open on her lap. I doubt if she even knows she's reading. Something tells me you could give this girl a phone book and she'd be happy.

"It's ah . . ." says Rosie, "it's um. . . . it makes me . . . I mean . . . I feel better when I read . . ."

Well, that was obvious, wasn't it? What's Neat going to do now? Kiss her with the duck? Nothing would surprise me.

"You know what?" says Neat to no one in particular. "Mr. D likes Rosie. So do I."

A huge, beaming smile spreads across the girl's face and she starts to blush.

This is banal TV with a loony edge. There must be at least twenty people out there who'd be enjoying this crap. A stumbling girl who reads obsessively, an ex-TV star who is stuck in questions mode, and my loopy brother. Phil sidles over to me and whispers loudly: "Isn't this great?" He's got to be kidding. "Man, it's cult TV," he continues. "I couldn't have dreamed up something like this if I'd tried."

"Why would you want to?" I ask.

He gives me a funny stare, like I'm a mental case,

then goes back to the girl with the headphones and whispers in her ear. She laughs quietly before shooting a quick glance over at me. I wave, trying my best to smirk despite the sick feeling in my guts.

You bastard, Phil. You're all bastards, exploiting my brother, selling a faulty promise to the desperados who watch your station. I just wish this would come to a quick and painless end. Maybe I should leave, wait in the foyer with my friend, Miss Poopy Mood. I glance around, trying to calculate the quickest exit, when my heart nearly skips out of my body. Over in a corner, lost in the shadows, is Todd. How did he get in here? When did he arrive? God, what the hell does he want? Does he want to speak to me? Is this payback time? Revenge on the bitch from hell? Why can't he just telephone instead? My head is swimming, and the room looks lopsided. I stare hard at the set again, hoping that the mundaneness of Neat's show will bring me back down to earth. Neat is placing Mr. D in the terrified girl's lap.

"You know you can do whatever you want to do," he says to Rosie. "Mr. D knows that too. He can see the real you, Rosie. Don't be afraid."

The girl looks like she's about to cry, but the camera has moved on to the couch where Lucky is asking quiz questions in a totally emotionless voice. Neat is touching the girl tenderly on the arm, and I feel like an eavesdropper, standing here with my oh-so-cool expression.

I chance another look at Todd, who is smiling broadly, like a father with a small child—*his* child, *Fat Boy Saves World*, the television event he helped create in my kitchen. He understands what's going on between

Neat and this girl. He belongs here more than I do. I feel intensely guilty for what I did to him, then I hate him for making me feel guilty. It really is time to go. The door isn't too far away, and I move toward it, slowly. Hey, this will be easy, just walk out, escape the nasties. But he'll watch me, won't he? He'll think I'm piss-weak. I won't give him that pleasure.

I can hear Phil rabbiting on about next week, then the kid with the guitar plays some music. It sounds like the show is ending. Now the studio lights are out and the crew are gathering, shaking hands and congratulating themselves. Todd hasn't moved, but I catch him giving me a quick glance. I look back at him, trying to be enigmatic—that should annoy the crap out of him. Anything, just to get this over and done with. Force him to come over and say what he has to say, then I can go. He's checking me out, seeing if I'm going to bite or not. Well, so what if I do bite? He'll just have to put up with it.

He's approaching now, slowly, like he's counting his steps. I can hardly breathe. Bloody hell, I'm not scared of him, am I? He's here, so close, eyes meet eyes, once so innocent, once so trusting. He's shaking, either that or I am. Okay, out with it, I'm ready. I know what you want to say. I dumped my entire history of crap onto you. I bucketed you when you were probably the only person in the world who bothered to try and be my friend. You could have helped me. You could have got through my defenses. Can't you see I had to cut you out? He moves suddenly, edging past me, mumbling, "I'm leaving," and I'm momentarily stunned.

No way is he getting away with that, walking out like a wounded hero! He's got to get it off his chest, let go of me so I can go on living.

I say, "Me too," and chase him out onto the street. He looks back briefly, so sure I'd come after him. I follow him, locked into his stride, his hurt, his bloody injured eyes. I have to do this, follow his lead until my guts stop churning and my heart stops falling apart.

He's telling the story for now.

Todd

Todd watched the tiny TV lights in the studio switch off one by one, leaving the job of illumination to a few fluorescent tubes which cast a murky green pall over the scene. It had been stupid to come—he'd realized that the moment he'd seen Susan. This was meant to be his celebration, to watch Neat's first show. He thought the place would be crowded, that he could blend into the background unnoticed. And since the only way out was past Susan Bennett, he was trapped.

A group of people gathered around Neat, slapping his back and shaking his hand. The fat boy seemed to be paying them no attention, all his focus on the girl, Rosie. She had such a beautiful, raw expression on her face as she looked over at Neat, so squat and passive next to her.

What had he done to this girl? Todd wondered. Told her the duck liked her. That couldn't explain the way her face had opened up. There was something else happening, something familiar to Todd, the memory strong in his heart. He'd felt it another time, in Goodman's room when Neat had cradled the sick man in his arms. He supposed it had been worth coming just to witness that again.

Todd shifted his weight from one foot to the other. It was time to leave. Susan was watching him from her lonely spot by the door. He chanced a quick look at her, sussing the mood. She had a lopsided, uninterested look on her face. It was so ludicrous. She looked like a bad actress trying to be meaningful.

What a farce this is, Todd thought. He counted to five, drew in his breath, then started for the door. He almost made it out, but for some idiotic reason he looked up as he reached the doorway and locked eyes with Susan. She wasn't going to look away, and neither was he.

The pause between them was excruciating, a great knot of misunderstanding.

Eventually Todd blurted out, "I'm leaving," and pushed past her. She said, "Me too," behind him and he almost ran to the front door of COMM TV. He burst out into the street, shutting the door behind him, only to hear it open again.

What did she want from him? Was there something she'd forgotten to mention in Goodman's room? Another detail to add to her sorry list of accusations? Todd tensed, waiting for a taunt or a scream, but he was followed in silence.

It was a strange game of tag. Susan matched Todd's footsteps, maintaining an even pace behind him, their shadows dancing together, puppets of the passing streetlights, receding then catching up. Todd watched the dark shapes as they embraced like bumbling clowns, tumbled away, then embraced again. He smiled, accepting the mood of the dancing shapes, and decided to throw in some absurd variations to their dance, like crossing the road, then crossing back again. She simply followed. So he stopped, bending to tie up his shoelace, but she just waited. He swung around a lamppost and she walked right past it. He ran his fingers along a corrugated iron fence but there was no counterpoint from her.

She's not up to it, thought Todd. She couldn't join in the living improvisation. It was like she was limited to repeating the same action over and over. He suddenly felt totally in control. This was his improv now, his call, and he would take it as far as he could.

They finally came to familiar streets—Todd's old stamping ground, only a few blocks from the boarding-house. He picked up speed, then turned suddenly down a laneway and stopped at a rusty iron gate. He heard Susan stop behind him, her breathing hard. He smiled, then turned to her and said, "I'm hungry," before pushing the gate open and picking his way carefully along a cracked concrete path. They arrived at a kitchen door, and he entered without hesitation. Susan followed.

The kitchen was a bustle of activity. Italian women sweated over boiling pots, the smell of tomato sauce and garlic overpowering the senses. The women paid no attention to the pair as they made their way through the kitchen and into a dining room. Several wooden tables lined the walls, each decorated with a plastic cloth, a bottle of cordial, glasses, and a basket of bread. Vases of plastic flowers topped off the effect. The place was almost full, and Todd quickly sat at the only empty table. Susan stood at the door awkwardly, as if she might leave now, after following all that way, and Todd said as lightheartedly as he could manage, "I'm going to have dinner. I don't know about you."

She sat down opposite him, her face alive with a thousand questions. Todd smiled; she was still in the drama, still improvising at her own pace. How much further could he take it? He poured them both a cordial, then leaned back on his chair and waited, never once taking his eyes off her.

It was her turn.

"Okay," she said in a deadpan voice. "What the hell is this place?"

"It's the restaurant with no name," explained Todd. "Highly illegal. They operate on word of mouth. One of the Theater of Possibility mob brought me here. What do you think?"

"Amazing," she said, ice-cool.

A teenage boy with a snarling complexion of pimples and craters arrived at their table.

"Yeah?" he asked insolently.

"What have you got?" asked Todd.

"The clap," the boy growled. "What about you?"

Susan nearly choked on her cordial.

"Me?" said Todd. "I've got hunger pains so I don't need waiter pains."

The waiter smiled, appreciating the joke. "Okay," he said. "We got spaghetti bolognaise, spaghetti bolognaise or spaghetti bolognaise. What you want?"

"I reckon two spaghetti will do us," said Todd. He handed over five dollars, then grinned at Susan as the waiter left.

"Don't you love this place?" he said.

"It could grow on me."

He sat back and waited, not sure where to take their interplay. Perhaps he could pretend that they were just two friends out on a Saturday night for dinner. That there was no past between them. No history of acrimonious slaps in a dim little boardinghouse room. They could enjoy the ambience, eat the meal, and not worry about messy things like feelings.

Great spaghetti . . .

Hey, wasn't Neat's show amazing . . .

I like your shirt . . .

Want to see a movie after . . . ?

It struck him that she might very well go along with that pretense, that she was comfortable with ignoring her feelings. The ice-cool Susan with her barrier up was enough to convince him of that. But it would be an ugly scenario, packed with lies and secrets and festering emotions.

Todd sat back in his chair. The improv was beginning to go flat. He had no energy for false dialogue and silly gestures anymore. Besides, he already knew that the rules kept changing with Susan. That no matter how much he thought he was in control, he'd wind up getting hurt.

The waiter brought two bowls of pasta, plonking them unceremoniously on the table. They ate in silence, looking around the room to avoid each other's gaze.

Todd wondered why she had followed him. Did she want to be with him? That was too funny even to contemplate. To hear something from him? That struck a chord. Perhaps she wanted the truth from him, the words that would define the mess they had created. Well, he didn't have them.

All he had was the power of gesture, of action, of reaching out at the right moment—that was the magic he trusted. He could try to reach out to Susan, to crack that frustrating barrier and see her sparkle again. It was a dangerous path to take, and if he was sensible he'd forget about it. He'd sit back and wait for her to self-destruct. But common sense was an area he wasn't too hot on.

Instead he opened his mouth to speak, and at the same time reached out to her.

Susan

Let him have his smile, his fun with the waiter, his little games out in the street. His pathetic follow-the-leader designed to make me look stupid. And it *was* stupid to follow him this far. God knows what I was thinking. I wanted him to get it all off his chest, to grill me on toast, but he won't, damn him! He's just sitting here eating his spaghetti, doing a deep and meaningful. Rage, damn you! Meet me and do battle until it's dead, that tiny flicker in your eyes that reaches out to me. Start a war and I'll kill that spark, then we can all go home and forget this ever happened. Forget about my fat brother who is trying to save the world, forget about my crazy head that can't stop being angry, forget about the way you tried, when so many before you gave up. He looks up from his pasta, ready to speak. It's about time.

"What do you want, Susan?" he asks.

Oh, come on. You're going to have to do better than that. "Parmesan cheese," I answer, "but they don't seem to have any."

"Great." He sighs.

Something tells me he wasn't expecting me to talk about cheese. Good. I'll give him more. "You'd think an Italian restaurant would have Parmesan . . ."

"Do you really want to talk about cheese?"

"I don't know. You tell me."

"No, Susan, you tell me," he says, raising his voice. "What the hell is it you want?"

That's more like it. A rise in the temperature, but not boiling yet. He's so gentle, so kind, that I'm going to have to work overtime to bring him up to battle speed.

"Ooh, temper temper." I smile, sitting back, waiting for him to bite. Todd obliges.

"What is it with you?" he yells. "Are you afraid I might actually like you or something? Or are you just afraid full stop?"

"Come on, Toddy," I say. He needs encouragement. "Let it all hang out."

"No," says Todd, standing abruptly. His bowl spins wildly on the tabletop, threatening to fall to the floor. Todd touches it gently on the rim and it sits back. Then he leans forward, so close to me, almost touching.

"I won't play," he whispers, and walks out of the restaurant.

You bastard! You shriveled-up little coward. Come back and fight!

God! I'm crying again. A group of Italian gentlemen look at me and whisper behind their hands, but I know what they're saying. Silly little bald-headed prima donna, fell for a boy who made her scared. Tried to kill him off but he wouldn't play by her rules. One of the old Italian guys is waddling over now with a hanky, for my tears. I take it and wipe away the evidence of my passion.

"*Amore*," he says.

"Yeah, whatever," I reply.

Amore, hatred, anger, fear. Hell, they're all the same as far as I'm concerned. Todd is right, I'm a mess of fear. It takes guts to do what he does, to stick with crazy girls even when you know you could get hurt. I haven't got guts. All I have is his question burning in my brain. *What do I want?*

Todd

Through the busy kitchen, past the sweaty Mamas and the boiling pots, into the backyard. Away from Susan, away from the game, time to let his head clear again. He liked it out here, in the cool night. The vast emptiness of it made him feel light-headed, detached from the earth beneath his feet. In his fancy he floated from the ground, out into the void of darkness. He bounced around the rooftops of the run-down cottages, buffeted from chimney to chimney. Cut loose! He was cut loose. But his fancy was broken by the sound of a voice, her voice.

"I don't know what I want," she said.

"Yes you do," returned Todd.

"How would you know?" It wasn't an accusation. It was a genuine question. How would he know? Because he had seen it in her heart.

"Just speak to me, Susan. That's all you've got to do."

"You're asking for too much," she said.

He turned now to look at her. The gray, shadowy features of her face, so familiar that they frightened him.

"I don't think you even realize how much you're asking," she said.

"I won't ask for anything."

"Then what am I supposed to say to you?"

"You'll know."

"Tell me!" she shouted.

"No."

She squeezed her eyes shut, the tears seeping through the barrier. With a cautious movement, Todd took a step closer to her. Just a step—the rest had to be up to her. He could smell her, the sweet odor of this girl. She looked up toward the sky and whispered, "shit," then closed the gap between them. They stood this way for a moment, touching, leaning into each other. He didn't try to put his arms around her, didn't try to take the moment any further. Feeling the rise and fall of her breathing, taking in the contours of her body, he was joined for this brief moment with the shadow, and he shook with the emotion of it. Shook like a freezing man or a frightened child, shook so hard that she shook with him. Finally the wave passed, and he was still, at peace. More at peace than he'd felt in months.

Then Susan broke the embrace, stepped back with her arms around her chest and said to no one in particular, "There's this stupid story in my head . . ." A long pause, then a quiet mumble, almost as loud as a heart beat. "You might like to hear it."

Neat

Where did they come from? All these scribbles daubed across the faces of others? Did they come from the past?

That must be it. They are nothing but salty ghosts left over from a long time ago that he eats without blinking. They don't scare him the way they seem to scare the others. Sitting here in his kitchen, with Lucky staring blankly at the refrigerator, Neat suddenly realizes he isn't scared anymore.

Fear has gone.

Why had he been scared in the first place? He couldn't remember. Did people frighten him? Was it pain, noise, anger? Perhaps it doesn't matter, now.

Then he sees his sister banging a cupboard and swearing loudly, and thinks he might remember. A little girl who loved him. A yellow duck they played with. Happy stories, happy stories, until someone took it away. Until he changed and changed and found out that he could see things no one else could see.

Like the little girl's face, here in the kitchen, where he sits smiling at nothing.

Susan

When I was twelve I went to the agricultural show with Lucy, a girl I knew from school. I wanted her to like me. No, that's not quite accurate. I was desperate for her to like me, to approve of me, to say I was okay. She came with her family to pick me up, cruising slowly up our gravel driveway in their station wagon. I ran out to meet them so they wouldn't have to see my family. The sixteen-year-old, silent brother, with acne and fuzzy hair on his bloated face. The father who always looked old, reading some ancient book in his study, calling out, "Is that you, Susan?" absently, but not really expecting an answer as I slammed the door behind me. The mother away at an art gallery opening, sipping champagne and small talk.

The show ground was dusty, noisy, full of a boisterous crowd. I felt out of place that night, and I kept losing touch with Lucy and her family. It soon became a problem for her, especially as she had to keep backtracking to find me and missing out on her fun. Eventually we came to the rides—the noise so deafening, the lights so thrilling—and suddenly I was there. Right on the spot where you could taste fear in the air. My spirits lifted immediately. We stood among the screaming thrill-seekers and I wanted to scream along with them. There was a ride behind us, a suicidal structure called Krazee Kat. That was the one I wanted, but Lucy wasn't keen, so I begged, and in the end she agreed, probably because she wouldn't lose me if I was locked in a ride.

At first Krazee Kat took us through the guts of its structure, slowly building up speed, gradually throwing us at wilder angles, turning us around at sharper speeds. Up and down, around turns, crazier and crazier, with us screaming all the way. Then our little car climbed to the top. We were on a long straight track that led toward the edge. There was nothing beyond the edge, no way out. Just emptiness and a long drop to a horrible death. Krazee Kat had gone from the predictable to the terrifying. Some sort of psychopathic maniac must have designed this ride. We picked up speed, hurtling toward oblivion. I was certain that in the space of a couple of breaths we would fly over that edge and die.

What a way to go.

What a story to tell Todd on that night together, standing awkwardly in a strange backyard, the feel of him still on my skin. Because Krazee Kat wasn't the first story that came into my head. I wanted to tell Todd another story, one about my eighth birthday, but I chickened out. I suppose they're connected in a way, those two stories. One set the other up. Todd wasn't to know that; he just listened with a slightly puzzled look on his face. I wonder if he thought I was talking about life, that I was telling him about Krazee Kat as a sort of clue to the twists, turns, and sudden movements of Susan Bennett? Perhaps I was.

Lucy and I were sitting in that tiny little car on a collision course with the wide open space of nothingness, and I realized with a sudden jolt that the idea of going over the edge excited me. I was injected with the energy of the ride, an insane madness that would fling innocent children into terror. This was the taste I'd wanted so much on the ground. The ride into chaos. Bring it on. Let's go! Over the edge and into disaster. Let it fly.

Come on! Come on! Here it comes! Now! Now!

Then we turned a bone-crunching corner and flew down a steep decline. Still on the track, still safe, everything okay. Was I disappointed? Not as much as I was relieved. I completed the ride in a daze. When we stopped, Lucy turned to me and said something banal like: "Wasn't that fantastic?"

I burst into tears.

Todd was very silent after I'd told him the story, and eventually I laughed and told him he didn't have to say anything deep or meaningful. He looked relieved. If he thinks that was a scary story, what about my first choice? Let him have Krazee Kat; it's good, safe stuff. We can chew over it during long conversations on the telephone, the instrument by which we conduct our relationship. Todd rings, I chat away, we hang up, then Todd rings again. I'll give him one thing, he doesn't let go. Since that awkward night he must have called me thirty times. Don't get me wrong, I want him to call. I need to hear his voice probing at me, gently pushing each day, trying to get a bit more of Susan Bennett out of me. He says he doesn't trust telephones, too easy to conceal yourself behind a voice. He'd much rather be with me in the flesh, so to speak, but I'm holding him at bay.

We stick to my witty observations for now. Little stories about my brother, or the state of father's liquor cabinet after one of Goodman's midnight raids, or the lack of food in the cupboard, thanks to another of Ponytail

Phil's visits. The spin doctor of community TV has taken to dropping in so he can chat about the show, staying on for a protracted afternoon tea that stretches into dinner.

I'm staring at the wreckage of last night's banquet, strewn across the kitchen table, spilling like modern art until it stops at my brother. My fat Buddha, sitting serenely as I rage around him, trying to find something to eat. Some kind of change has come over him since he did the first episode of his show last week. He seems so bloody happy now—he even smiles. He never used to smile. Well, maybe once, a long time ago, when stories were safer, before my eighth birthday.

Neat doesn't seem to be interested in my stories, not with the world to save. He's only interested in other people, other places. I wonder how I look to him? Am I transparent, an invisible object that cleans up the mess? He won't save me, my fat boy wonder; I'll look for that elsewhere. I got a taste for something in that backyard, a desire I haven't dared to have before. In the shake of Todd's touch, in the softness of his voice.

If I don't fly over the edge into disaster, if I don't banish those innocent eyes again, if I can keep my secrets locked away and still enjoy his touch, then I'll meet him somewhere and just be next to him. Perhaps we won't talk. We could take a leaf out of Neat's book, be silent for a change. That would be easy.

We'll meet and be ordinary, for the sake of harmony ... and Todd ... and awkward embraces that make my skin tingle for days.

For the saving of Susan Bennett.

Todd

Statistically, *Fat Boy Saves World* had doubled its audience appeal since the first episode last week. There were ten people waiting in the foyer to be part of the live television experience of the decade. Todd counted the small "crowd," living proof that somebody, somewhere, watched community TV.

He was due to meet Susan here. She was late. He'd found excuses throughout the week to ring her, chatting away about nothing. Doing a slow, circling dance that was both exciting and excruciating. Relishing his new role as Susan's confidant and friend. Pushing gently for more, because he could see that so much more was hiding behind her evasion.

Like her self-conscious little parable about madness and show rides. At the time, Susan's story had struck him as being a bit too carefully constructed. Was he supposed to see her ride on Krazee Kat as a symbol for her life? All through her telling he grappled with this nagging doubt that this girl, who was extremely clever with words, with stories, was playing with him. Could this be a little test? Was he supposed to offer some sort of wise response? He decided to just shut up and listen. When she came to the end of her story and told him how she'd cried, he saw the raw energy and emotion that she bottled behind her words. He saw again that she was a girl who could take him beyond the boundaries of safety, where joy and terror danced hand in hand. To a place where he had to act on instinct alone, because there were no scripts to guide him, no tried-and-true lines to follow. His heart beat faster just thinking about it.

It had been his idea to meet today at Neat's show, and she'd been reluctant at first, said she didn't want to spend another afternoon locked up with the weirdos, but Todd insisted. He felt safer meeting here, out in public. There was less chance of being blown away by her stormy eyes.

Besides, he liked the so-called weirdos and freaks; they were almost like family to him now. Over near the toilet door a group of four kids stood waiting. Dressed in black, their hair gelled to a fine layer, they smoked cigarettes elegantly in between outbursts of giggling. The girl, Rosie, was back from last week. Several other lonely-looking people filled the gaps, each of them clutching a soft toy—two teddies, one rabbit, and one dog.

Rosie was beaming, shooting glances at the corridor that would lead them to the TV studio when the show began. She was a different person from last week; her downcast look was gone and her hands were free, no book to be read over and over. Todd wondered if this was because of Neat's téte-à-tête with her last week. Whether his words had somehow given her the strength to move on.

A new punter entered, and Todd recognized him as the kid who'd played his guitar during the first episode. He took up a position against the wall, next to Todd.

They come back, Todd thought. They come back to add fuel to Neat's performance. Fire meets wood, heat plays with air, and then it rages.

Next to him the guitar kid stretched, then spoke in a surprisingly deep voice. "Do you smoke?"

Todd shook his head.

"Neither do I. Gave up last week," said the kid.

"Right." Todd nodded.

"What's he done for you, then?"

"Pardon?"

"The fat boy," said the kid, as though Todd was some kind of imbecile. "He helped me give up the suicide sticks. What about you? I seen you here last week."

"Oh, I'm not here . . . I mean . . . I'm sort of meeting someone . . ."

The kid laughed, a deep, throaty growl. "Relax, man. It's okay."

Todd knew what the kid was thinking. That he was too afraid to talk about his "problem," the one he'd brought to the fat boy. He tossed up whether to explain to this kid how he'd been the one to get the whole show happening in the first place. Even back then he hadn't been looking for answers. He'd wanted amazement, shock, excitement and life—he wanted that desire in Neat's eyes. And what did he end up with? His own desire burning in his own eyes.

"You're not going to say it, are ya?" said the kid.

"What?"

"Why you come here. You know, what you're lookin' for."

"I'm looking for my friend," said Todd. Then he grinned, adding, "Actually, she's why I come here, you know? She's what I got out of the fat boy?"

"For real?"

"Yep. Look around, you might find a friend here too."

He left the guitar kid with that thought and went outside to exchange the smoky air of the foyer for the grimy air of the city. A taxi pulled up, and Todd recognized the bulk of Neat in the front seat, hands out in front of him as if to keep the dashboard from squeezing him further. Lucky Goodman sat at an awkward angle in the backseat like a discarded mannequin, but there was no sign of Susan. Was she coming separately? Todd went over to ask Neat, but Phil intervened, almost hysterical at the lateness of the fat boy's arrival.

"We go to air in fifteen minutes! You've got to get here earlier next time. Where's your sister? Is she paying for this taxi? Or am I supposed to?"

The fat boy waddled past the frantic Phil and on into the building, a vague draft of air his only answer. Phil tore the money from his pocket and paid the driver, then ran after Neat. Lucky Goodman shuffled along behind them.

Todd waited impatiently on the footpath, looking for Susan in every passing car, searching up the road for an approaching taxi. The COMM TV foyer was almost empty now; everyone had filed into the studio. What had gone wrong? Did Susan chicken out? If he went to her house now, would they pass each other along the way? He went into the studio, hoping the show would distract him from his rising sense of doom. It wasn't much to ask of her, just to come and see what happened next. Why was life so scary for her?

The audience was crammed in behind the couches today. A girl in headphones yelled out that they were on air in "one," meaning one minute. Phil was standing by with the microphone, ready to do the introduction, pacing up and down, and Todd recognized the preperformance nerves. The girl with the headphones gave a ten-second countdown and they were on. Episode two of *Fat Boy Saves World.*

It began the same way as last week, with Phil giving the potted history of Brian Bennett, miracle boy who emerged from his silence to save the world, then Neat taking over the microphone. He had a brief chat to Rosie again, then the fat boy talked to a couple of the new fans. Phil stood in the half-light, just out of the set, watching his demented chat show in progress. What the fans had to say was fairly unremarkable, but then, Todd found an awful lot about the show unremarkable. He wondered if that was its appeal: a sort of antidote to the slick, modern presentation of most TV. So many of the faces around him were smiling, even the four gel-heads, and Todd became aware of his own detachment.

Now the camera had moved on to Lucky Goodman and the ex-quiz-man froze, in stark contrast to last week's performance. There was an awkward silence, filled by a few giggles, then Goodman started to moan. It was a familiar sound to Todd. He closed his eyes and winced at the memory of it. Neat waddled over to the old man and held him, whispering furiously into his ear. The camera operator didn't know what to do, looking out from behind the viewfinder at Phil. This was TV at its most embarrassing. Eventually Phil intervened and gave a quick rundown of the coming attractions on COMM TV while someone led the moaning Goodman out of the studio—away from the place where he might be saved.

Neat stood by, looking confused. There was something different about him today. Todd tried to pin down the change. He almost gave a yelp of shock when he realized what it was. There was no Mr. D—Neat's hands were empty. The duck wasn't lying around the set, either. This was wrong, very wrong, and Todd began to feel panic. Was this connected to Susan's absence?

He went out into the foyer, but the place was empty. Alone, the faint aura of disaster around him, Todd felt the safety barriers move again. Where the hell was Susan?

Susan

The last time I looked at this wall, there was a thin line of black ants making their way home across its boring surface. They were my brother's entertainment. He was staring at them, I was staring at him. I thought he was a silent blob, but he spoke. A miracle in the city mall! A bloody hoax, more like it.

I've had a phone call from my father—perhaps a long time ago, or just now—I can't tell. It has propelled me into my brother's room, where I sit mutely, staring at the wall. I feel myself about to cry again and I hold on to it. Not yet, I'm not ready to let go yet.

It's not so bad here in Neat's bedroom, the afternoon light is quite pleasant, and the bare walls are a welcome change from the splashes of art in the rest of the house. I could get used to being here, the new silent member of the household. And why not? Being silent in my family has many advantages. How else would you gain affection, love and attention around here? What better way to be noticed by an author stuck in his head? By a mother dotty about visuals and struggling artists? This is not the million-dollar question I am posing here—the answer is deceptively simple. You stop talking. Easy, isn't it?

When I was little, I used to come to this bed every night to fall asleep. In my brother's room, where a fantasy boat that could sail me into the land of dreams waited for me. Here I was warm, here I was safe in the arms of my brother, captain of my nocturnal voyages.

Each night my mother would tuck me in, looking distractedly around at the state of my room before giving me a dry peck on the cheek. "Goodnight, darling." I can even remember the sound her kisses made: a tuneless "smack." But I needed more than a dry peck, I needed cuddles and stories and promises of starlight. I needed love. And I found it with Neat. I'd wait for a while, then crawl into his bed, to be greeted by a mumble or a murmur. A slight shuffle, even a whispered "good night," before I fell into my sleep. It never once occurred to me that my parents didn't know where I was. I knew. I was in a warm bed where I could snuggle up against the silky smooth skin of my brother-pillow and drift off to sleep.

It was so innocent, so comforting, and it was shattered on my eighth birthday. My father bursting in, seeing his son naked with his daughter. Thinking twisted, nasty thoughts that had nothing to do with our sleepy selves.

I wonder what Neat would make of that now, my savior of the world? Could he save me from the pain of that night? Or save himself? Because that was the night he stopped speaking. The night he turned into my father's freak show, the character from a book, the silent boy.

And all through his silence I believed that my nighttime captain was still in there. That he still loved his little sister and would one day return to cuddle her again. What a joke. Instead, he's betrayed me.

Of course, it was my father who carried the news of Neat's betrayal. Funny how it always seems to involve him. I was on my way to the studio, having shoved my brother into the front seat of the taxi. Neat took an age to squeeze in, trying to ignore Goodman's foul temper. The old man had been in a bad way ever since I hid the booze from my father's cabinet. I was about to get in too when I heard the phone. For some reason I thought it might be Todd, a last-minute change of plan or something, so I sent the others on their way and ran inside.

I wasn't prepared for the faint echo that crackled down the line or the background hiss of an international call. I heard my father's voice bouncing along the fiber-optic cables and into my head.

"Hello? Who's that?" he asked.

"It's me, Susan."

"I'm sitting here with a fax in my hand," said Father, his anger veiled behind the deep voice. "It's a clipping from the newspaper, Susan. Sent to me by a well-meaning friend. Do the words *Fat Boy Saves World* mean anything to you?"

"Yes," I sighed, not wishing to play his game. What did he expect me to say? That I'd never heard of it? Had we become so used to lying to each other that he even offered me opportunities to do it?

"I won't bore you with predictable phrases like 'What the hell is going on over there?' because I doubt if it would help my mood at the moment. I'll just say this and say it once. The show has got to stop. Not next week, but now. I won't have Brian being made an object of ridicule. I'm amazed that you let it happen in the first place."

I let it happen? It had nothing to do with me, it was Neat's show, his call. He's the one who took Phil in with open arms, the one who waddles around the studio with bizarre recipes for salvation, who holds disgusting old men in his arms and whispers to them. My mind twisted around these facts, the insanity of the past few weeks— my walking, talking, fat-bear boy who chose to be the TV Messiah. And it was in the middle of this tortured reasoning that I stopped. Chilly fingers of doubt lashed around my throat, expanding, squeezing, shaking me violently, until the realization hit me.

My father didn't sound surprised. There was not a hint of shock in his voice. No amazement that the silent boy was not silent. No terror at the imminent destruction of his international reputation. Just annoyance that the fat boy might be laughed at. I heard myself tackle him, asking, "Why, Daddy, why? Why aren't you surprised? What do you know?" He answered me with silence, the background hiss of the telephone line building to a crescendo. Finally, his voice again, small, the boom vanished.

"Susan. I thought you knew."

"Knew what?"

"I just . . . I presumed that Brian had told you . . . because he was speaking to you . . ."

"What?" I yelled.

"Brian has been speaking for some time now . . ."

"How long?"

"Don't, Susan. It's not worth it . . ."

"How long!"

He sighed. "About two years."

Two years ago. He knew the significance of the timing. Two years ago was when he packed me off to boarding school. Two years ago was when he had finally had enough of his troublesome daughter. What sordid little secret was going on in my family then? Were Neat and Daddy-dear holding private conversations across the hall about me? Got to get rid of the sister. She's mad, she's crazy, she talks too much.

"You bastards!"

"Calm down, Susan," he said. "Not even your mother knew at that stage. It was kept very quiet."

"Why?" I spat. "So no one would know that your book was a fraud?"

"Susan, it was very private work I was doing with Brian. I had no idea if it would be successful, or even if it would last. I had to follow Brian's cues."

"Why was I kept out of it?"

"That's not for me to answer."

"What?" But I knew what he meant by that. In my heart I knew too well. It was for the other one to tell me, the so-called silent boy. My brother. I'd fought long and hard for him when no one else cared. I was his champion. He'd betrayed me. He cut me out like I was nothing.

"You still there?" asked Father, after a long pause.

"Yes."

"I'm sorry you had to find out like this."

"Bullshit. Two years ago. Was it before or after I went to boarding school?" I was up to battle speed now, ready to fight. No way was I going to let myself cry on this phone. I wouldn't give him that pleasure.

"What does it matter, Susan?"

"Before or after?"

He didn't answer, but his silence told me everything. I've become an expert at reading silence.

"You got rid of me because Neat was speaking."

"That's not true . . ."

"Of course it's true."

"Susan, you left us with little option about boarding school. Surely you remember what was going on? That letter you wrote to the newspaper, 'My father's book is a lie,' and I had to sweet-talk the bloody editor so he wouldn't publish it. The goddamned interview with the German magazine. You faked my answers. You and I were at war, Susan."

"Truth is the first casualty of war, isn't it, Dad?"

And daughters are the second. He shunted me off because I might spoil the party. I can't remember much of the rest of the call. I hung up on him, I think, then came in here. I have this urge to trash Neat's room, smash it into pulp, but I'm afraid if I do that I'll lose control of the warrior-woman for good. That she'll take over my life completely.

I've got to get out of here. Out, out now. Away from this room, away from this house, away from the warrior-woman before she kills someone. Onto the streets, through the traffic, "up yours" to the cars if they honk their horns at the crazy girl dancing down the main street. Screw them. Got to hail a taxi, go, get in, and say the words that might lead me to a safe place where I can be held.

"COMM TV studios, Campbell Street, city."

Neat

He takes the microphone, that loud instrument, and speaks to them. "I know this is hard," he pants. It must be hard for them, stuck behind the scribble of the past. If they can eat it away, then what amazing things they would see. The world so clear, so young.

"Sometimes there is a lot of pain . . . and you got to . . . you swallow it," he continues. "I did it. You can do it." He puts down the microphone and goes over to a wall next to the set. Picking up a can of gold spray paint he squirts out giant words, as big as mountains, marching across the wall: Eat the Pain.

"You can do it," he wheezes, his breath fading away. "Like this."

Then he swallows for them, takes great gulps of air.

It's a simple demonstration. "Eat the pain. Eat the past, take it all in." So simple, but they don't believe him.

There are a few shuffles of feet, a few whispers, but nobody copies him. Why is it so hard for them? Why can't they just gulp it all down, then it will be out of the way? He looks around for the duck, to use it as a demonstration, then realizes it's not there. That it lies stuffed inside a pillow at home, hiding its face from him. So he won't be able to see them, those other scribbles, that other past.

Behind him the gold paint drips down the wall, the words losing their meaning, stretching and distorting with each roll toward the earth, until they become mere decorations.

Todd

Through the glass front doors he saw Susan's taxi pull up and smiled with relief. She hadn't chickened out after all. As Susan stood on the footpath, paying the driver, Todd watched her every move—the way she leaned forward, the angle of her head, the loop of her arm on the taxi's roof. Somehow they didn't add up. She seemed crushed, damaged, knocked out of her skin. It was shocking to see her this way. His first instinct was to hold her tight, ask what had happened, but he stood back, meeting her at the door instead.

"Are you okay?"

She looked up like a dreamer waking from a sleep and said, "What?"

"Susan, what's wrong?"

"It doesn't matter," she said, defeated.

"What do you mean?"

"It doesn't matter!" she shouted. "Nothing does now. It's over, all of it. This stupid TV show, Neat's dream, your dream, they're gone. Finished. It's finished. Don't you get it? Finished. I've just had a phone call from my father."

She slumped against the wall and slid herself onto the floor, her arms around her bald head, hiding from the world. Within seconds she was crying.

Her sobs nailed him to the spot. He was unable to respond, not even with a step forward. Why was this happening again? How many more times would he have to face this storm? Was there ever going to be a normal moment?

The thought came to him that he should rush down to the studio to ask Neat what to do. But what would the fat boy say? Would he tell Todd to look at Susan in the same way he had looked at Rosie? Or suggest he cradle her?

Todd knelt beside her and listened passively as her sobs mingled with the sounds around him—his own breathing, the traffic outside and the faint noise from the studio, where the world was being saved. He hated feeling so stuck, it was as suffocating to him as a pillow to the face. He had to act, to move, to touch, but he was terrified of the consequences. The stakes were higher now, there was more to lose.

He touched her tentatively on the shoulder but she pulled away. So, he couldn't touch, and he couldn't act, and he couldn't rely on his instinct.

"Susan, what do you want me to do?" he asked.

"Nothing," she said, her voice muffled.

"Come on . . ."

"Why the fuck are you asking me?" she asked, lifting her head. "I knew this was a mistake."

Then she stood, ready to go, but he stood with her and held her arm.

"Let go!"

"No."

She struggled to break free. "Let me go!"

"I won't. You came here to me. I won't let go."

"You had your chance and you did nothing."

"What was I supposed to do?"

"I don't know!" she raged. "Make it up. That's what you do, isn't it?"

Not here, not in this situation. He couldn't make anything up. "Just don't go," he said. "I can help. . ."

"Don't bother. No one can help me. I should have realized that in the first place."

She turned her head away from him, but she didn't try to go. Todd saw a slight easing of her stance, and in that moment he felt his mind start to work again. He couldn't rescue her, he couldn't save her from her demons. She wasn't a character from a play, to whom he could magically say the right words and suddenly she'd be smiling. That script didn't exist. All he could do was stick with her, no matter how much she protested, until she saw that he was going to stay.

The sounds of a guitar and scattered applause came from the studio; another twenty minutes of world saving was over for the week. Within minutes the foyer would be filled with strangers. He had to get her out of here.

"Susan, I can't help you. You're right." He registered the shock in her eyes and went on quickly before she took what he was saying as an excuse to vanish. "Because I'm not in there . . . in your head. No one is, only you. But I'll walk with you."

She rolled her eyes and tried to pull away again.

"I know it doesn't sound like much, but really . . . it's all I can do right now. Besides, this place is going to fill with Neat's audience any minute. Will you come with me?"

Now it was her turn to say the right words. To give the answer he craved.

To say yes.

INTERLUDE
NIGHT SWIMMING

Susan

If I dive down deep enough in this soupy water I will vanish. Down where it's cold, where the only flavor is salt green and muddy. Where I can open my eyes and take in the subtle shifts of gray and black.

I'm not alone down here.

Another body swims around me, a pale shape that occasionally comes near, sending streams of little bubbles past my face. I could breathe in those bubbles, take their air away, or I could choose to breathe for myself.

This is my first experience of the peaceful darkness of night swimming. Secure in my underwater envelope, I rise to the surface. It is still here, quiet, the stars peeking through clouds. I roll over onto my side and swim long strokes. A white blur flashes past the corner of my eye, a hand caught in the moonlight. Suddenly the water before me erupts and I'm swamped by a small wave. It fills my mouth with the bitter, salty taste of the sea. From somewhere beyond the frothy waves comes a raucous laugh. The attack continues, more and more waves, until

I retaliate, pushing foamy brine at the dark shape. It screams loudly, then dives to avoid the assault.

Todd likes to play games.

We arrived at this seaside swimming pool after many hours of arguing and talking and testing each other until the limits ceased to exist. Coming from his bleak confession in the COMM TV foyer to this, playfully splashing. I know it won't last forever. By the time I get home I'll feel angry again at my brother. But that's in the future, and it's the present I'm swimming in now. Night swimming.

Todd eventually persuaded me to leave COMM TV and come with him. I would have run, I wanted to go, but in the end he got through to me. Just a little, a tiny crack of light, but it was enough for me to follow him out onto the street. He hailed a taxi, and for some reason took us down to the harborside. He was terrified, I could see that on his face. Stuck with this howling, wet-nosed, dribbly-faced girl on a Saturday night. We sat on a low wall and listened to the sounds of the city across the harbor. The distant streetlights were dancing on the water, doing the shimmy, doing the shake, stuck in a sixties time warp. I threw in a rock, trying to break them up, but they kept dancing. Todd sat quietly, watching me try to obliterate the go-go dancers on the water. In the end I gave up and turned on him, shouting at him, demanding to know why he was there.

"Why? I've been a bitch to you. I've treated you like shit."

I can't remember his response exactly. It was calm at first, then angry, but even that didn't satisfy me. Shouting brought no release, and crying was worse, so we sat in silence again.

My mind kept racing over the past, trying to work out where I had hurt Neat. Because I must have hurt him, otherwise why would he betray me like that? After all those years of speaking out for him, of being his "special," his little Susan. I couldn't understand it. Perhaps Todd could, so I told him the story of my eighth birthday.

"I remember I was telling Neat about my favorite present," I said to him. ". . . Can't even remember what it was now. Then the door opened. My father came in, his voice . . . God, it was so loud. 'What the hell is going on here?' And he pulled back the covers . . . I was cold . . . Neat was shivering . . . naked. Me trying to pull back the covers again but my father's arm . . . rough and immovable . . . 'Get out of there now!' he shouted. I was terrified."

I knew what Father was thinking—Todd did too— but it was entirely innocent.

"They sent Neat away after that," I told Todd. "I don't know for how long."

The memory of that empty time came back to me. The confusion of my eight-year-old brain. I knew I must have done something terribly wrong, because I'd made Neat vanish. And when he came back he wouldn't speak—not to me, not to anyone.

He lied to me.

I wanted to scream that phrase, smash those buildings across the water into pulp with my voice. Maybe, when I was eight, I should have screamed with terror, or for sheer release. I might have come through a hell of a lot better. I might have even been able to live with my father's international fame, the adulation of a man and his book, when I knew in my little girl's mind that he was the one who had made Neat silent in the first place. Perhaps I could have been normal, if only I'd screamed. Instead I chose to wage war on my parents. I raged and I battled, but none of it released me.

Either way, I guess I still would have come to this. Faced with my brother's deception. With the fact that he hid his voice from me deliberately. After I'd worked so hard to protect him.

When I'd finished telling Todd my story I asked, "Now what?" and he said, "We walk." I couldn't move, but he insisted, said it was time to get the energy going again. And he was right, the walking did help. I felt my spirits lift a bit, then we talked some more, but talk can't last forever, and Todd eventually suggested we go for a swim.

"What, now?" I said. "But I don't have a bathing suit."

"That's okay," he said. "I'll swim and you can watch."

Sometimes I look with awe at the way Todd attacks the world. We walked along the harbor for a while until we came to a wooden fence, which we climbed over easily, illegal intruders into a small seaside pool that is mostly used by old men and women with long memories and short breaststrokes. Todd stripped down to his undies straightaway and dived in, his body white under the fluorescent glare of the streetlights. I sat by the side of the pool. He taunted me, kicked water at my legs, but I wouldn't move so he swam away. It felt so lonely out there on my own, beside the water, the observer, the silent commentator, the watcher. I was sick to death of being lonely. The moon came out from behind some clouds, and a white dancer appeared on the water, shaking in time with Todd's spirit. I took off my jeans and sat back down, watching the dancer do the go-go. She slowly drew me in, piece by piece, into my watery haven. I was expecting Todd to splash me, but he stayed back and waited until I'd dived down deep, until I'd had my drink of solitude. Then he attacked.

He's swimming around me now, some sort of demented dolphin, surfacing every now and then to make feeble "ee, ee" noises. He dives, and his arm brushes lightly against my thigh as he swims beneath me. I gasp with the shock of it, a private reaction to a private sensation. Touch. Did I mention touch? How it had vanished from my life along with Neat's conversation.

Even though my father and mother eventually realized that nothing had been going on between Neat and me, that Father had overreacted, touch was banned from that night on. I'm sure nothing was said, they just stopped doing it. Apart, of course, from quick little hugs for goodbye and the odd dry kiss. My rations.

I haul myself up onto a pontoon and lie in the cool air, enjoying the way it tickles my skin. Underneath, the gentle bobbing of the floating wooden structure cradles me with the rhythms of our water-fight game. After a while Todd pulls himself up out of the water and lies down behind me, causing the pontoon to rock from side to side. I can hear his breathing, still heavy after the swim, then his hand touches my arm. God, it's so warm, I can't believe how warm it is. I let him leave it there, too afraid to move in case he takes it away. It's funny, a few hours ago I wanted to rip his hand to shreds for touching me.

"Do you hate your dad?" he asks after a while.

I close my eyes. Sometimes there are no words for what I feel about my father. "It's not really as simple as that."

"Na," he laughs. "It never is."

"What about you? Do you get on with your dad?"

"Not really. My old man used to call me a 'bloody poser.' That was when he was in a good mood. And my mom just used to shake her head and tell me they had special hospitals for people like me. She was joking, by the way. Pretty zany sense of humor, eh? But maybe I am nuts, you know, because lately I've been missing them heaps."

"Yeah?"

"I know, it's stupid, isn't it? I used to impersonate my dad all the time, do his country drawl for my mates."

He starts droning in a slow caricature of the country hick.

"People don't really talk like that," I say.

"He does," says Todd. "One day I was with a whole bunch of kids from school. We were in town, and I saw Dad in this shop so I did his stupid, dusty way of talking and the old man came out in the middle of my performance. Stood there, looking at me, then he got into his car. At the time I thought it was a huge laugh. Now . . . I dunno."

"Don't tell me you regret it?"

"Well, I do."

"You've gone soft." I laugh. "The city has made you soft."

"It's okay to be soft, isn't it?" he asks.

How can I answer that? To be soft you've got to trust people, and look where that can lead you. Broken, betrayed, or even happy with a warm hand on your arm. I thought I'd given up on trust.

"You'll just get hurt," I answer. "Softies always do."

"Mm," he says, rolling over onto his back, the warm hand vanishing suddenly.

"I should have been hard with Neat," I say, quietly, letting the words drift from my mouth like mist. They float gracefully for a moment, before falling to the ground.

"You believed in the story," he says, "and not the truth."

"That's very deep." I sigh, warding off his reply. "Does it actually mean anything?"

"I dunno, I just made it up."

"Oh, great." I begin to roll off the pontoon, but he stops me, hand on my T-shirt, holding me, suspending me in that moment.

"When people tell their stories . . . you know, in the theater . . . you've got to listen for the truth in the story as much as you listen to the words. Someone might say they want to conduct an orchestra, but really what they're saying is they want to be in charge, the big boss. It's like that with any story . . ."

"Even my father's?"

"Even your father's, even Neat's. There's a truth behind the story. That's what you've got to listen to."

Very helpful, I'm sure. I roll into the water before we can have any more deep and meaningful conversations. He dives in after me. We play cat and mouse for a while, pushing, wrestling, the odd hand landing where it shouldn't, our legs locking together now and then, our faces close. When I swim around behind him to grab him by the waist, he twists and protests and swivels until he is facing me, our bodies squeezed together, our eyes so close we look like blurs. We start to sink, slowly, and he takes a deep breath before pulling us under completely. In the murky darkness he reaches up and strokes my stubbly head. I lean my face on his shoulder, cradled for a moment in the still water. Then I pinch him hard and he lets go. Through a flurry of bubbles we rise to the surface gasping for air, my head tingling from his touch. It is excruciating; I want more but I can't, not yet.

"What?" he says, pulling back like he'd hurt me.

"It's okay." I laugh. "I liked it, really."

And I swim away, kicking water into his face. The swimmer's final revenge.

3

THREE ACTS
OF SALVATION

Extract from *The Silent Boy* by Peter Bennett, winner of the International Peace Prize for Literature

A religious man I know invited me to pray with him for Brian, to save my son's soul. I declined.

This is not a time for prayer, for kneeling at the altar of a distant deity. To me that has always looked like begging, and I will not beg.

I will hope. And my hope is that one day Brian will find his voice again, will unleash the flood of thoughts that are dammed behind his wall of silence.

Same outcome, you might say, just different means.

I'm not so sure.

If Brian spoke again it would be a salvation— the finding of a lost soul. But not a soul lost to the spiritual world of the pious and holy. Brian's is a soul lost to himself. Confused in a maze of his own creation, the dead ends and frustrating turns of his decision to shut himself off from those who love him.

Neat

He can hear the noise that fills Mr. Goodman's head.

He pleads with the old man, yells into his ears, urges him to rise out of his dark room for a second time. "Eat the pain. Gobble it up."

Don't let the stench of failure creep up on you, don't let the nasty night frights come and haunt you in your bed. Don't let the baddies come and chase you into a dark place. Don't let them turn you into something weak and sick, when you know that you are strong.

He says all these words to his friend as he lies in his hospital bed, but they bounce off like hailstones, rattling around until they become pure noise.

Noise the enemy. Noise the destroyer.

He panics.

How could noise get in here? He has conquered pain, past, words, and silence. Already he can hear his own brittle moments shattering like crystal.

People approach him, nurses in uniform, but they

are strangers with questions. "Who are you?" "Where do you live?" "Are you a friend of Mr. Goodman?"

"I don't know . . ."

Walking is a great effort, lifting his feet through the heavy earth, dragging his body through the crushing weight of life. It is a very great effort.

But he walks. He escapes. This feeling is so familiar to him. So sickeningly familiar.

Finally, somehow, he comes to the house. Upstairs is a room, a place to breathe again in quiet.

He is greeted at the door by a familiar face, Susan. Not the Susan who came home from her school, but the Susan of old. The one they sent away. How long has it been since he's seen her, with that wild, angry face? Was she in Mr. Goodman's room, hiding behind the door? Those burning eyes, that parade of indignation.

Susan tries to stop him. She asks so many questions. She never used to ask questions. He pushes past her with difficulty, up the stairs to the room. With a groan of relief, he sits on the bed. He is Neat, alone in his room.

He seeks the peace that only silence can bring. But the peace eludes him. He can hear the noise. The invader, it comes from a great distance, like a band of far-off children, howling and clawing at the world. Louder, closer, more insistent, until it is in his head. Even here in this room, the noise is in his head.

He tears at his hair, tries to rip his skull off to let the noise out, but it stays. He lies on his bed and weeps like a small child. Now he has nothing. Not even his silence.

Susan

It is creepy. It is pitiful. It is war.

A low, painful moan seeps out of my brother's bedroom. I run up the stairs and bang on his door. "Shut up! Shut up!" You won't get away with it, not the second time. You won't take the injured role again, the poor fat boy. My heart is hard and callused. I am her, the steely warrior-woman. I'll see him sink into the mud before I feel sorry for him.

The minute he walked through the door I yelled, "Why didn't you tell me, you bastard?"

His only reply was to stumble into his room and shut the door. That's when the moaning started and I lost it completely. I banged on his door; I clawed at the paintwork. The salty crust of peace that covered me after my night swim with Todd vanished. God, how long ago was that? Hours? Days? How long since I sent Todd home with a promise that I would stay calm?

Todd should see me now, still outside Neat's room, still lost.

"You're not going to win!" I shout.

This will be my mantra, my chant of strength. The long night slips away, the chill air slapping me awake whenever I feel dozy. He is silent so I wake him with a cacophony of kitchenware until I hear moaning. Then I'm satisfied. His anguish will help me stay awake a little longer. I have to do this, rage and battle against his shut-out silence. I have to make him meet me. Goddamn it! He will meet me and answer my question. He no longer has the right to hide behind the persona of the troubled, silent boy.

The dawn comes and I feel ready to be sick, but I won't give in. I bang on his door.

"Why didn't you tell me you could talk?"

Is that my voice, that pathetic warble? I slide down onto the carpet.

How many times have I shuffled past here, knowing my brother was inside doing nothing? It seems pitiful now. Waging war against my parents for driving Neat into silence, for lying about it. Waging war on Neat for a similar crime. I can't do it anymore. I can't turn my entire family into the enemy, it's just too hard.

Drained, my warrior-woman comes to the end of her battle. Her sword too heavy to hold, the mud too deep to wade through, she falls to her knees and cries, "Enough!"

He is quiet when I open his door. Perhaps he's fallen asleep. For a terrifying moment I think he's dead, but his enormous body shifts slightly at the sound of my footstep. He is lying facedown on his bed, buried in his pillow, a figure of despair. And the smell! God, has he soiled himself or something?

"Oh, Christ," I say dramatically, "what's that smell?"

It totally rattles me, the sight of him. He's a mess and his holy shrine of a room is even messier. I'm used to seeing my brother contained, neat.

He speaks to me through the pillow, a muffled little voice. "Who are you?"

Oh, that's a good one. Now he's forgotten who I am. "I'm Susan. Remember me?"

Then he turns around, and I nearly faint at the sight of him. So much pain and anguish and damage on his face. This isn't the brother I've had all these years. This is a sick parody of my Neat.

"I can't see you," he says.

"Why? What's wrong with your eyes?"

I move closer, but nothing seems to be wrong with his eyes. He can see perfectly well. He is focusing on me again, his head wobbling from side to side like it's hard to hold up. Eventually he asks me: "What do you want?"

What do I want? To rip him apart? To take advantage of his weakened state? To make him pay for his betrayal? None of that seems real anymore. I can't be angry with him, and I don't bother trying.

"I've come to help," I say.

But he rolls over on his bed and moans. From somewhere inside the pillows and tangled sheets I think I hear him say two words. "The noise."

Todd

"Bloody hell, Todd. What are you doing?" whispered Carrie.

She normally didn't speak during a performance, and Todd nearly dropped out of his role at the shock of hearing her voice. He gave her a quizzical look, then Natalie whispered in his ear that he had the character wrong. He glared at her. Wrong? What did she mean, wrong? It was a guy wanting to ask this girl out on a date, wasn't it?

"They already know each other," said John through gritted teeth as he continued being a "dancer" in a night-club. How the hell could they know each other, thought Todd?

He must have missed something along the way, again. It had been like this ever since he'd left Susan the other night. He wondered if he might be having an out-of-body experience. A sort of detachment between his spirit and his flesh. Like a ghostly image from a badly tuned TV set, he would put his coffee cup down, then feel it happen a few seconds later. His problem was with connection—to the outside world, to his body, to Susan's history.

It worried him how Susan could hold on to emotions from years ago. Stuck in anger at her father, fear for herself, outrage at the debacle of her eighth birthday. They seemed like lead weights to Todd, heavy memories that held her down, the building blocks of a rigid structure. It was no wonder Susan seemed hidden behind a barrier, that he could only get momentary glimpses of her through the cracks in the wall. He wanted to make more cracks, to dig and chip and smash away at the structure until it collapsed in a heap. The night swim had been a good start, their little interlude of normality between the dramatic "highlights" of Susan's life. Like what was happening in that house. Has she confronted Neat, yet? What was the outcome? These questions were his obsession, his distractions from the here and now.

Carrie's voice called out through the drama. "Act three. Scene change to the bedroom."

This was Carrie's latest idea, breaking their performances into acts like traditional theater. Calling out, like a god from the wings, whenever she thought things should be moving on. He wasn't comfortable with this artifice; somehow it seemed foreign to their form of improvised theater. Carrie said it gave the performances more structure, but right now it just made things more confusing. It was act three already, and he had no idea what had happened to act two. He shrugged mentally and hopped into the bedroom scene, half guessing what he was supposed to say and do. He hoped it might make sense to the audience. It was so foreign to him to be detached from a performance like this. On the stage was where he usually felt the most alive, the most connected.

But his spirit was elsewhere—in that house, wondering what was happening between Susan and her brother. He winged through his role, half guessing, half taking cues from the others, until it was finally over. The other actors were furious, shooting glances at him as Carrie wrapped up the performance. He didn't waste time with their anger; he could deal with that another day. Packing his kit quickly, he waved goodbye and walked out. Someone called after him that they should have a debriefing but he ignored it. Stuff them, he thought, they have bad performances too.

He practically ran to the bus stop and managed to catch a bus straightaway. He had agreed to leave Susan alone for a week, to give her the space to work it out with Neat. But it was torture playing the good boy when every fiber of his body wanted to be with her, not stuck on this bus.

The traffic was heavy, the bus was slow, and each stop

added to his sense of frustration. Old men and scrappy kids took their time to disembark, and Todd wanted to yell at them to hurry along, as if they were stuck in the same molasses he had been moving through these past few days. Finally the bus arrived in the city, and Todd jumped from the top step onto the footpath, showing the slowpokes behind him how it was done.

He jumped over a rose garden, half ran through the small park, and ended up on the street where another bus headed for Susan's suburb. He told himself he would just go and look at the house, make sure it wasn't on fire or there weren't any bloodstains running down the door frame. That was all. Then he'd go home satisfied.

He took his seat on the bus, his mind running through a hundred imaginary conversations with Susan. They were all the things he would say to her in the perfect situation, those unreal circumstances where just the right words could change her life instantly. He would say that the past was just a story, that you had to tell it and retell it until you began to understand it. Then you could go on living. He would tell her to move on before she forgot how to breathe, before her whole life became set in the rigid concrete of regret, anger and misery.

The Bennett mansion seemed very normal when he arrived. No bloodstains or screams from the distance. No signs of a struggle. Todd stood for a mere second watching it, then he walked up the drive. There was no way he could stand back and observe, not now that he was here. He rang the doorbell several times but there was no answer, so he tried the handle. To his surprise, the door opened.

The house was still, and Todd entered the marble hallway, calling out, "Hello." He was on his way up the stairs when he heard footsteps. Susan was standing on the landing, a mildly surprised look on her face.

"You'd better come up," she said. "Neat's in trouble."

Then she turned and was gone. Was that a ghost Todd had seen? She was so distant and pale. He ran up the stairs and tried a few doors before coming to the right room. Neat was lying on the bed, his face buried in a pillow. Susan was on the floor, her back against the bed.

"I did that," she said, indicating Neat with a flick of her head.

"What?" asked Todd. There didn't seem to be any obvious signs of damage on the fat boy.

"I drove him away," moaned Susan. "Just like Daddy did. I'm no better. Neat's gone again."

Todd went and shook the boy, but there was no response.

"Neat. Neat. It's me, come on. Roll over. How's Mr. Goodman? Is that the problem? Is he all right?"

There was a muffled "No" from the pillow.

"He's been like that for days," said Susan. Then she added dramatically, "It's like my eighth birthday all over again."

"That's crap," said Todd.

Susan sat up and glared at him, outraged.

Much better, thought Todd; at least she looks half alive now. He spoke quickly, making his point before she had a chance to kick him out.

"Susan, he's talking. Listen to him. It's nothing like

your eighth birthday. He's still connected, he's responding to questions. You haven't done anything to him."

"So, what's wrong with him, then?" she asked.

"Not sure." Todd shrugged. "Where's Mr. D?"

"What?"

"The duck will get him out again. It's got to be here somewhere. Neat didn't have it in the studio last Saturday."

Todd started searching through the bedroom and Susan watched. There was no sign of the duck in Neat's room, so Todd tried the rest of the house, but the search was hopeless without Susan's help. He came back into the room, wondering if the duck might be the key to unlocking Susan's despair too. Mr. D was so significant to Neat, perhaps he'd once been significant to Susan as well.

"God, I wish we could find that duck," said Todd, gauging her response. "It's like, he never lets it go . . . it must mean something."

"Do you think so?" she asked.

"Yes, but you'd know better than me. I mean, you used to play with it as kids, not me."

She seemed shocked. "God, I suppose we did. There's so much I don't bother remembering anymore."

"Susan, what happened when you came home?" asked Todd.

"I started yelling at him . . . and he wouldn't answer so I banged pots and scratched at his door, and he went so quiet that I came in and found him like this. I was scared . . . you've got no idea. I thought . . . when he wouldn't move . . . I did some awful things, Todd."

"You were angry."

"I'm so sick of being angry."

"Okay, then don't be angry," said Todd.

"I wish it was that simple . . ."

"Why isn't it?"

She laughed, shrugging her shoulders. "I guess I'm programmed to be crazy."

"That is so frustrating," said Todd. He stood up and paced around the room, wishing he could shake her out of her mood. But it was too hard. All his imaginary conversations, his clever lines deserted him now that he was with the real Susan. She sighed and he turned around to see her staring at Neat. She still thinks she's killed him, thought Todd. How was he going to talk her out of that one?

Then, to Todd's surprise, Susan smiled and shouted, "I know!"

"What?"

But she didn't answer, going instead to the head of Neat's bed and searching inside one of his pillowcases.

Eventually she came out with the scruffy duck. "Voilà! One Mr. D. We always used to hide it there. I'd forgotten."

Todd wanted to yelp with joy, not because she'd found the duck, but because she'd broken out of her heaviness. It gave him a burst, just to see her like that, and a thousand ideas ran through his head. "Show him Mr. D," he said.

"No," she answered. "He knows I've got it." She stared at the duck for a while, then said quietly, "I've got to do this my way, Todd."

"That's fine," said Todd.

"Alone."

"Oh . . . I mean . . . of course. But what if . . . ?"

"Please, Todd."

"Okay," he said, realising he was out of it for now.

"It was sweet that you came. . ." she continued.

"Don't kick me out," he pleaded. He couldn't stand to be away from her for a second time, not knowing what was happening. "I'll stay downstairs, out of the way. You won't know I'm there, but if you need me I will be. Okay?"

"Okay," she said, after too long a pause.

He left then, reluctantly closing the door behind him.

The fridge was nearly bare downstairs, but he managed to scrape together some food which he ate at the table, stopping to listen every now and then. All was quiet upstairs. He went into the lounge room. There was still no sound from Neat's room, and Todd grew restless and bored. He turned on the TV to distract himself, but there was nothing on but crap. Eventually he switched it off and lay down on the leather lounge, wondering how anyone could possibly make furniture so comfortable. It didn't take long before he drifted off to sleep, his long days and nights finally catching up with him. He slept so deeply that any dreams he had were buried under a great darkness. Out of that darkness he heard snatches of conversation which grew louder and louder, until they became sharper, closer, a slightly hysterical voice. A woman's voice.

"Peter, we've been robbed. My ashtray, the silver sculpture, the candlesticks . . ."

Todd opened his eyes. It was dark now, and a light spilled in from the front entrance. A light he hadn't switched on. The woman's voice continued to list missing items, and Todd began to realize that it didn't come from his dream but from the house. He sat up and blinked a few times, scratching his head as the woman's voice stopped. Then he heard another voice, a man's, close and deep.

"And it would appear we have company, Bel."

Todd looked up as a silver-haired man with a ramrod-straight back entered the room.

"Good evening to you," he said. "I'm Peter Bennett. And who might you be?"

Neat

He hears the duck's voice.

Through the noise and torment he hears Mr. D call him by a name he hasn't heard for years. "Calling Captain Neat."

How could this be? He thought that name was lost forever. When did Mr. D remember it again? Slowly he rolls over, like sand moving, grain by grain.

"Hello," says Mr. D.

Hello, duck, he thinks. And hello little Susan, somewhere there, hiding, playing peeks behind her hand. He didn't think little Susan would ever come back, either. His warm young friend who used to whisper, "Take me away, Captain Neat." And he would sigh, allowing the sleep to come and smother him with a blanket of dreams.

Maybe the duck can help him with the noise. Or little Susan perhaps? If he could dream, the noise might go away. If he could stop thinking about bad times and noisy fights and remember how to float, the past might break up into bite-size chunks that he could gobble down again. Help me, little Susan, he thinks. Help me swallow the pain, help me see the scribbles.

Then he remembers how little Susan went away. How she was never coming back again. Never, never, never. Too mad and cross to ever come back. She's gone, gone, gone away for good.

That was sad, and he asks out loud, "Where did you go, little Susan?"

Susan

"What?" I reply.

It is such a strange question, straight out of left field. And what does he mean, "little" Susan?

"I went to boarding school," I say but he shakes his head. "Well, what do you mean? Where did I go when?"

He starts to moan, turning his body away from me.

"No!" I shout. "Don't. Come back."

Then I hold the duck up and speak in the voice I've been using. "Come back, come back." I don't know if it is the voice we used when we were young but it brought results before, got Neat to turn around and look at me. Even got him to speak to me and ask his weird question. Where did little Susan go? As far away as possible, that's for sure. Away from her scary father who didn't like what she did at night. Away . . . like Neat went away. God, is that what he means?

"Little Susan's here, isn't she? She's holding me," I say, courtesy of Mr. D.

He turns back to me, studying my face for a moment, then shakes his head. "Maybe. She's tricky."

Who, me? Or little Susan, or both of us? God, who knows? I certainly don't. Does he want me to be like I was at eight, is that it? Too late, buster. The eight-year-old has grown up, shaved her head, and screwed up her life, all in the space of a few weeks. Not bad going, eh? If he wants a Susan, he's got to take this stubbly-headed one. I'm right here with a duck in my hand, wondering what has gone wrong with my boy-mountain. Perhaps I should just ask him. It's worth a try.

"What's wrong with you?" I ask via the duck.

"You know."

"Tell me anyway."

"The noise."

There it is again. What noise? Must be in his head; all I can hear is the distant sound of the TV downstairs.

"Where did the noise come from?" I ask in my own voice, but he just closes his eyes and gives a little whimper.

"I want to dream," he says, his eyelids fluttering like a dainty maiden's.

Well, that would be nice, wouldn't it, just to drift off and sleep for a while? I could do with a bit of respite too, but somehow I don't think it will be possible, with this enormous mountain of misery waiting for me. I've got to get him out of this. I was responsible, despite what

Todd says. I wanted this to happen, or at least the warrior-woman in me did. God, she can get me into some messes, like the time I slapped out her rhythm on Todd's face. But, hey, he's still around, and so is my bloated bear. She can't be all that bad. For a brief second I have this crazy thought that she can help Neat out of this, but somehow I don't think so. He wants the little Susan, Miss Cutesy with the gaps in her teeth and the nonsense about sailing to dreamland on a boat.

Well, maybe I could give him the little Susan. Don't know how I'll do it, but maybe it would work. I laugh at the thought of it, me speaking in baby talk, asking Neat to be my captain. I don't think so. Something simple, that's more my style, a gesture or act that doesn't require me to be a total idiot.

I throw back the covers of Neat's queen-size bed and say, "Move over, lump. Here comes your little Susan." He doesn't budge a centimeter, so I squeeze in, half of me suspended over the edge, the other half squashed up against his soft, flabby body. It's quite warm under here, even a bit cozy. I close my eyes and try to remember what it was like in bed with Neat when I was little. Is this how it felt, half squashed, warm?

"Okay," I say to Neat, "is the little Susan here now?"

He rolls over to face me, the blanket sliding off me in the process, and stares for a moment before shaking his head. Great, I'm not the little Susan, I'm the big Susan. What do I do now? Suck my thumb? I don't think I ever did that when I was young anyway. This is so ridiculous, my leg has slipped out of the bed and is touching the floor.

Here I lie, a contortionist, twisted into this bizarre shape because he is too bloody stubborn to move. This bloody great lump of flesh that has always been in my life, blocking the view, standing in the light, squashing my toes, and all with a serene look on his face. Except he's not so serene now, more dewy-eyed and pathetic. I wouldn't be surprised if he started whimpering. Then what would I do? Scratch him on the tummy like a dog? Throw him a bone? A fit of giggles rises up from my belly, and I stuff my fist into my mouth. After all, this is serious. Well, it would be serious if it wasn't so hilariously insane.

I must look absolutely stupid, a bald stick figure squeezed next to an overinflated bladder. Rolling over with my fist planted firmly in my mouth, I squirm with laughter, an hysterical bodysurfer about to be drowned. Here it comes, the wave, the wave, and I explode in a thousand places, burst out loudly, raucously, until I'm engulfed in laughter. It shakes the whole bed and I turn over to Neat, but the sight of his loose face muscles wobbling up and down crack me up even further, so I look away. That's when I see the duck. That bloody duck! It's so dopey with its bright blue beak and cacky yellow face, and its slightly insane eyes. Tears of laughter pour out of me. Everything is stupid, everything is funny and everything is wet.

"Oh God," I gasp through spasms of laughter. "I've . . . I . . . bloody . . . wet my . . . self." He nods, perhaps he has too.

"That's better," he says, and I agree. It is heaps better to laugh. Wetter too, but even that's okay. So is lying here together, stupid, but okay, laughing until my stomach muscles threaten to tear. After a while my head stops spinning and I manage to breathe again without choking.

Neat makes little grunting noises, and starts lurching away across the bed until I have space enough to lie on my back. Ah, comfort at last. I let out a sigh and Neat sighs too.

"That's better," he says again, then he closes his eyes.

I keep mine open, staring at the ceiling, brief wisps of the past floating above me. Like my secret giggles in his bed after one of us had let off a smell, or my silly little songs that I used to make up out of nothing, or how I used to wake in the middle of the night to find his arm on my back.

Neat starts snoring next to me, and I give him a nudge in the ribs. Even that feels familiar. I smile and pull the blanket up over my face, closing off all the crap that happened outside our cave, in the past. Now I can finally allow my eyes to shut, now I drift into half-sleep—half-waking, where the most amazing color dreams flash past. But they are so elusive that the minute I try to remember one it vanishes completely. I doze like this for quite some time, in and out of color, until a gentle knocking comes at the door.

"Susan," calls Todd.

"What is it?" I ask, my voice still dreamy.

"Susan, your parents are here."

I blink, running through what he just said. Did he really tell me that my parents were here? Am I still dreaming? It seems so stupid and I call out, "Bullshit."

"Really. Your father wants to see you."

I sit up and stare at the door with Neat snoring peacefully next to me, the absurdity of my situation hitting me like a rocket. It's the craziest thing I have ever heard—my father is outside the door. So I do the only sensible thing. I scream.

Todd

Todd panicked and threw the door open, Susan's father hot on his heels, both yelling in a simultaneous reaction to her scream.

"What's happening?"

"Susan?"

Todd was in the lead, eyes wild, seeing Susan upright in the bed and Neat slowly rising. He paused momentarily, but Peter Bennett didn't and they crashed in a tangle of legs and arms onto the floor. In the brief moment of silence that followed, Todd thought he might die with embarrassment, lying there under the bulk of Peter Bennett. He felt so stupid breaking into Susan's private moment like that, a bumbling buffoon, an intruder. He couldn't look at her, he just wanted to melt into the carpet. Then she laughed. So freely, infectiously, abandoned, wild and delightful. Todd craned his neck up, her face was so fresh, and he grinned foolishly. "Total idiot at your service," he said, trying his best to bow, on the floor, while Peter Bennett climbed off him awkwardly.

Susan flopped back onto Neat, lost for the moment in laughter, and the fat boy grinned openly, pointing to his father, saying, "You're back."

Susan's father brushed his slacks down and said, "I really don't see why this is so funny. You scared the living daylights out of us, screaming like that."

Then Susan's mother came in saying, "What happened? What happened?" until her husband waved her off distractedly, and said, "Everything's fine. I think." He took a step closer to the bed.

"Susan, please, will you stop this now? What was wrong before? Why the scream?"

His only answer was more laughter. Todd went and sat at the end of the bed, enjoying the air around Susan and Neat. So much had changed since he left the room an hour or so ago. They were connected now, and Neat's face seemed to be relaxed, open again. The fat boy was back. Eventually Susan stopped laughing and looked at Todd.

"Is that one of your better entrances then?" she asked.

"The worst, more like it," he said, blushing.

"So Mommy and Daddy, you've met Todd?"

"Yes we have," said Belinda Bennett.

"Really, I think we should talk," her father said. "I don't like any of this. Strangers in the house . . ."

"Todd's not a stranger," said Susan.

"And. . ." Susan's mother interrupted. "There are items missing. I was very close to calling the police."

"Oh Mom, what for? So they can come and arrest Todd for being my friend?"

Susan's mother gave a curious half-smile. "When everyone's ready," she said, "we will talk downstairs. It's more comfortable there." Then she left.

"Poor Mom," said Susan to Todd. "She can't handle messy scenes."

"Okay, Susan," said her father, a clear note of warning in his voice, "I thought we could do this in a friendly way. I didn't want trouble."

"Do you realize how many times you say that to me?" she asked.

"Please," he sighed, "I don't want a fight."

"I'm not fighting. I'm just saying it as a matter of interest. You must have said it ten thousand times—'I don't want trouble,' and we always ended up having trouble. Funny that."

"Yes, okay, Susan. Whatever you say. How are you, anyway, Brian? Getting on all right? Did Verena treat you okay?"

"I'm saving the world," said Neat.

"Oh . . . yes . . . I wanted to talk with you about that."

"Come on, Todd, let's leave them to it."

Susan hopped out of the bed and led him by the hand. He liked the feel of her skin, was disappointed when he had to let go for the narrow stairs.

"Daddy is such an interesting chap, don't you think?" she said lightly.

"He's old," said Todd. "I never realized he was that old."

"Yeah, they had us kids when they were half-ancient. He always used to say, 'I'm too old for this.' It's another one of his fave lines."

Something told Todd he might be hearing more "fave" lines fairly soon, judging by the way the father and daughter reacted to each other. They hadn't seen each other for weeks, months, and already they were sparring.

Susan's mother was in the lounge when they entered, throwing open all the curtains and windows.

"The place needs some airing," she said. "It's so stuffy. Like something has died in here. Now Susan, your hair. Did you do that by yourself?"

"All my own work," said Susan, rubbing her head. "You like it?"

"I think it's . . ."

"Don't bother, Mom. I know you hate it."

"Honestly, Susan, you don't make it easy, do you? Shaved head, Brian in some strange TV show, you're playing truant from boarding school, important works of art are missing, and Verena seems to have melted into the woodwork . . ."

"The candlesticks are in the toilet," Susan sighed, interrupting her mother's litany.

"The toilet! What are they doing in there?"

"I thought they'd look good," she called out as her mother dashed out of the room to rescue the hapless candlesticks.

Susan sat back in the leather lounge and sighed, her face tired now. Todd touched her on the arm lightly, shocked at how quickly her light mood had vanished.

"You okay?" he asked.

"Yeah, just gathering my strength. You don't have to hang around, you know. It would be fine if you wanted to go, really."

"No," he said, a little too forcefully. "I want to stay. I

couldn't bear it . . . not being here . . . not being with you."

She blushed and took his hand in hers. "That's what I like about you. You stick around."

"Is that all?" he said, and she laughed.

It was a relief to see her laugh again. They sat for a while, listening to her mother rattle around in the background, fixing things.

"This might get ugly," said Susan, and Todd nodded. He'd seen a little bit of it already.

"But not you," he said.

"Oh yes"—she shuddered—"even me. Don't say I didn't warn you."

They heard her father's footsteps. As he breezed into the room Susan gave Todd's hand a quick squeeze and whispered, "Here we go."

Susan

"Come back here at once, Susan! Do you hear me? You can't just walk out like this."

Oh, Daddy, Daddy, so melodious on the printed page, so predictable otherwise. Of course I can walk out. It's exactly what I'm doing now, walking straight out of the lounge room, through the foyer, up the stairs and into Neat's room.

It didn't take long for the old familiar scrapping of the Bennetts to begin, kicking and clawing as only we know how. The first shot was fired when Father tried to evict Todd, and I said, "If he goes then I do too." We circled after that, shooting the odd arrow, testing our strength. The next salvo came when Father snapped off about the TV show again, blaming me, not listening to what I had to say. Poor Todd, I could feel him squirming in his seat next to me, waiting for me to say, "It was his idea, not mine." I wouldn't do that; he doesn't deserve to be thrown into this mess.

I waited until my father had exhausted himself with accusations and recriminations, then I calmly told him that I also thought *Fat Boy Saves World* was a terrible idea. He stopped on the spot, eyeing me suspiciously, like "What's she up to now?"

"It's sheer exploitation," I said. "A tiny community TV station getting free publicity out of Neat. It's a cynical exercise, as far as I can see."

"Then why the hell did you let it happen?" he asked.

"Because I wasn't in charge; Neat was. It's his baby through and through. That's a bit hard for you to swallow, isn't it?"

"Susan, I can accept a lot about Brian, but I cannot agree that he knows what he's doing with this TV show."

"Why?" I asked. "Because you're not in control, is that it?"

"Don't lecture me about trying to control Brian—you of all people."

"What do you mean?"

"He was your just cause, Susan, your weapon to use against me. You raged and rebelled in the delusion that you were championing Brian, but precious little of it had anything to do with him. It was all about you."

"Crap!" I yelled. "It was all about justice. Because you

would never acknowledge that you had anything to do with his silence . . ."

"Oh, not that birthday story again." Father sighed.

"Oh yes, Daddy, that birthday story again, that piece of history you would love to write out of everyone's mind."

"Susan, this is not going to help the situation, or Brian for that matter."

"Since when have you ever cared about helping Neat?" I spat. "You've always treated your son as a useful career move."

"That's not fair!" he shouted.

"No, it's not fair, is it? You snatched up Neat and made him one of your characters. He was like your doll, that you wouldn't let me play with. You kept him all to yourself, even had your own little secrets with him, like when you wouldn't tell me he could speak again. And you blamed that on Neat, but that's crap. It was all your doing. That's why this TV show is getting up your nose, isn't it? You think it's my idea. You think that Neat and I might be having our own little project away from you. You can't stand that, can you?"

The whole room exploded then, with my mother yelling her version of events, my father defending himself and me reveling in the noise. The only quiet person in the room was Todd, who looked terrified. That used to be Neat's role, silently watching the family self-destruct. The fighting Bennetts, doing what we do best, tearing ourselves apart.

Then it hit me like a smack in the face. In the middle of the firestorm, the truth hit me. We'd been doing this on and off ever since my eighth birthday. We'd been fighting over who owned Neat, and none of us did. What a joke. I thought I was being Neat's champion, but it had nothing to do with him. My burning banner, my holy war, it wasn't for the silent Brian Bennett, it was for me. *I* wanted to fight and battle. Instead I should have done what I did in Neat's bedroom earlier. Laugh . . . scream . . . release. That's what Neat meant when he wanted the little Susan tonight. She didn't bother with war games, she just lived whatever she was feeling.

I had to walk out then, leaving them all to it. My mother and father frothing at the mouth; Todd freaking out at being left alone with them. It was so clear to me what needed to be done.

Up the stairs I go, the playful mood from my giggles on Neat's bed echoing in the background, blocking out father's outraged shouts for me to come back. Neat is sitting on his bed. He's probably been listening to us, and I take him by the hand and lead him into Father's study across the hall. It is the only room with a lock on the door.

The first thing I do is turn the international award to the wall, for my sanity's sake. Now it's gone, I make myself comfortable, here in this place of lofty literature where the "great work" was invented. Neat licks his lips in anticipation. Perhaps he knows something has changed in me. I take the time to look at my brother, through my "now" eyes, my changed eyes, my eyes that no longer see the enemy everywhere. How many weeks is it since I looked at him in his bedroom and thought I was seeing the whole of him? The fat boy, sitting motionless, staring at ants. What did I really see then, in that pause between in-breath and out-breath? Did I see my strange roly-poly brother, my neat brother, my silent emptiness? Deep silence, empty silence, silence without meaning, silence that says it all.

God, how easy it is to load up the simple act of not talking. To assume and presume and take advantage because silence is a "nothing." But silence screams when it wants to, silence pleads, silence makes powerful statements. He is not crazy, my brother. He is not retarded or damaged; he is unique. He has a face that displays the pure essence of himself. That's what Todd was trying to tell me all those moons ago in my kitchen. I can see it now, glimpses of it. He is without a mask. He is Neat. How did he achieve that? By not talking? And what do I look like to him, my brother, with his eyes shaded by nothing, by silence?

What does he see?

Neat

"Tell me what you see," she asks.

He can see her face, flushed and bright. He can see a red flame burning behind her head, her banner. He can see that she fights to be strong, but that it burns her up as well.

"I'm sorry I tried to destroy you," she says, but he doesn't feel sorry.

He doesn't feel destroyed, either. He feels good because the little Susan is in the room. He sees other Susans too. So many of them scribbling over her face with their careless noises.

"I can see everyone now," he says, "on your face," but she doesn't understand.

"Don't stop," she says, sitting forward, taking his hands.

He is startled by her touch, that raw expression of herself, transferred like electricity across their skin. When did Susan learn to do that? How much has she woken up? Perhaps she wants to wake more. Perhaps she really wants to know.

"Open your mouth," he says, and she does so. "Let it all go in . . . warm spaghetti . . . Chinese noodles . . ."

"Come again? Noodles? What's that supposed to mean?"

"It's your pain," he says, and her smile vanishes. The scribbles become furious, her face crushes and folds into itself. Then she cries.

"I've wasted eight years," she says.

"No, you're eating it now," he tells her. "And you have to eat to be strong."

She nods, opens her mouth, and the past goes down like a slippery fish, gobbled up by the present. By Susan.

Todd

"Well, I feel like a whiskey," said Peter Bennett. "Anyone care to join me?"

Todd was too stunned to answer, the raging argument still echoing in his ears. It wasn't until he heard

Susan's father rattling around the liquor cabinet that he felt the embarrassment of being left alone with her parents. Suddenly the author exploded, and Todd cringed.

"There's no whiskey!"

"Don't tell me they've stolen that, too?" asked Belinda Bennett. She shook her head, then looked at her husband. "Well, those boarding school fees are certainly worth it, aren't they?"

"Now, Bel," he said, "you can't expect the place to perform miracles. Susan is Susan . . ."

"Stuck in her own world," summarized Susan's mother. She started picking imaginary fluff off the expensive rug at her feet. "I thought you handled that birthday business very well."

Peter Bennett sighed, a tired, sad expression on his face. "Well, I've had years of practice."

Todd began to squirm in his seat. This was such a private conversation. Belinda Bennett looked at him and half-smiled, half-jumped at the sight of him. She turned to her husband, but he was working up speed now, building up his case.

"Why does she persist with that story?" he asked, anger growing in his voice. "Year after damn year, the same accusations . . . Taking her to counseling was a waste of money . . ."

Todd almost rose in alarm at the father's words. "Counseling"—what was that supposed to mean? A psychiatrist? Why, because Susan was upset, or because her father couldn't handle it? He was still ranting about his daughter, standing above the drinks cabinet, all thoughts of a whiskey gone from his head. Susan's mother broke into his soliloquy, giving Todd the briefest of glances. "Peter, I think perhaps another time . . ."

"No, Bel, I'm sick of it. Nothing happened on that darn birthday, and I don't care who hears about it. All those years she's clung on to this falsehood, some child-like notion that I made Brian stop speaking. For god's sake, what about all those psychiatrists' reports? Don't they mean anything?"

"Is there anything else to drink in that cabinet?" Belinda Bennett sighed in a last-ditch effort to end her husband's speech.

He bent low and surveyed the wreckage of his once-proud drinks collection. "They've cleaned me out. Must have had a few parties or something."

"No," said Todd, his voice almost squeaky. He had to speak, stop this bizarre scene where he was just a mute observer. Mainly because he wanted to leave, and manners told him he couldn't just walk out, not when they were so involved in their private conversation.

Peter Bennett wheeled around at the sound of his voice. "Pardon?" he asked.

Todd nearly froze on the spot. "Um . . . I don't think there were any parties," he said nervously. "It was Mr. Goodman who drank all the whiskey . . . and whatever else was in there."

"And who might he be?" asked Belinda Bennett.

Todd grappled with exactly how he could describe Lucky Goodman, the man with a thousand quiz questions. No matter what description he used, Lucky was going to sound strange to them, so he simply said, "He's someone that Neat saved."

"Oh, good heavens," said Belinda Bennett, standing up and stretching. "That's enough for me. My body says it's the afternoon, but my mind says it's bedtime. I'll leave you to clear up, Peter."

Todd wondered what she meant by "clear up." Get rid of him? Call the police? Or deal with the troublesome Susan?

"So," said Peter Bennett, lounging on a chair empty-handed. "You actually believe he can save people, do you?"

He looked like he was settling in for the night, and Todd felt stifled by his presence. All he wanted to do was go to Susan, to see how she was. Now he was stuck in a conversation about Neat, and if they were going to talk about belief and saving the world, it could be a very long conversation.

"Not save people," said Todd, "but I think Neat can sort of reach people . . . well, I mean . . . I've seen it."

"What have you seen?"

Todd gave a brief description of Neat in Mr. Goodman's room, the way the fat boy cradled the man, the way he went to him when everyone else ignored him. He went on to describe how Neat had helped Rosie with her obsessive reading. Todd didn't offer any explanations for these events, he simply told them as stories, letting them speak for themselves.

"And what was Susan's role in all this?" asked her father.

The white blur image of her hand about to slap his face flew past, and Todd blinked momentarily before speaking.

"It was exactly like she said . . . She didn't want to know about it. I mean . . . it was me who started it all in a way. I talked Susan into it. So I'm the one you should be blaming."

He regretted saying it the second it came out.

Peter Bennett didn't seem to care what role Todd had played. He scratched his chin carelessly. "It's funny," he said. "I'd have thought Susan would be supportive of Brian. That was always her role in the family. I suppose that's why she felt betrayed by his secretive speaking."

Todd was amazed; the old man seemed to understand fairly well what was going on with Susan, so why couldn't he say those words to her? Why did they have to yell and push and shove? The echo of their fight rolled across his consciousness—sharp words, spikes in the sound level, pitching, heaving, until it was gone. In the silence that followed he realized he was being asked a question.

"What do you do, Todd? School?"

"No," said Todd, shaking his head. "No, I'm an actor." Then he blushed at the word, how pretentious it must sound to this man, who had been all over the world. Who had probably met famous actors, stars of real theater—not some little company that played out other people's dreams in bare church halls or noisy amphitheaters. But if Peter Bennett was contemptuous of Todd's self-description, he wasn't showing it. Todd found himself being lulled into a relaxed, conversational state by Peter Bennett's questions, until he realized he had been the only one speaking. He talked about the Theater of Possibility, about Neat's appearance, how that was when his desire to save the world first materialized.

"And you didn't know Susan before that?" he asked.

Todd shook his head. It must have been ten or fifteen minutes since Susan had left the room. Would she be wondering where he was? Would she be sitting upstairs waiting for him? He looked up at the ceiling, his body language pining for her. Peter Bennett smiled and said, "I suppose you want to be with her now."

Todd nodded.

"Can I tell you something before you go? Seeing how you have been so generous with me about your life?"

What could he answer? He had to say yes, to sit through more conversation with the old man.

"Have you ever read my book?" Peter Bennett asked, and Todd told him he'd read some of it, that he was still finishing it, even though he had already taken it back to the library.

"There's a passage in the book where I take down all of the little signs I'd put up around Brian's room. They were prompts, if you like, my attempts to get him to speak again. I was giving up, at least that's what I thought I was doing at the time. But something happened to change the way I looked at it all."

He paused for a moment, lost in thought, and Todd wanted to hurry him up, move him along.

"It was late at night," said Peter Bennett, head slightly tilted up in recollection, a storyteller's pose. "I was walking past Brian's room when I heard a voice . . . his voice. It actually terrified me, but on the surface I was nonchalant. I almost walked on, explaining it away as the TV or something. But really I knew it wasn't the TV. I knew that I had arrived at the moment I had been praying would happen for all those years. You know, the strangest thing happened. I couldn't go in, I couldn't open that door. I just stood and listened. It wasn't fear that stopped me, it wasn't disbelief, it was respect. I would be violating his trust if I barged in on him, on this profound moment. Yes, it was respect that halted me at his door, and respect that probably caused me to tear down those signs. Respect for something I thought I hated—Brian's silence."

He paused again and Todd started tapping his foot, then stopped because it looked so obvious.

"I went to bed, but I couldn't sleep. His voice kept going through my mind. The next evening I hung around his room, trying to engineer a moment when I could 'accidentally' hear him speak, a chance moment where we could both acknowledge this change. It didn't come. Then one night his door was slightly open, and through the crack I saw what I'd been hearing for all those weeks. He was bent over, talking to something. At first I thought it was his hands he was talking to, then I realized it was a toy."

"A duck?" asked Todd.

"Yes. How did you know?"

"It's called Mr. D. Neat talks to it all the time."

"Yes . . . it was the duck. Mr. D, eh? What a strange name. Do you know, standing there, watching him speak to that duck, I wept like a baby. But still I didn't go in. I know it sounds crazy. I'd written a whole book about him, but it was about the silent him, the one who couldn't answer me back. This talking Brian was different. So I kept my distance, watching him whenever I could, hoping he might invite me in. Then the trouble with Susan escalated. I don't know what she's told you . . . anyway, eventually she left. The whole atmosphere in the house changed then, it was like there was more space around every object, every person. I found myself standing at Brian's door, then entering the room. It was as though some invisible force had vanished. I picked up the duck, asking him why he would talk to this but not to me. He just stared at me, silently. I kept at him, and slowly, unremarkably, he began to talk to me. About the past, about when he was young—mundane conversations that I cherished, so precious to me, each one a pearl. He never mentioned anything about wanting to save the world. I wonder where that desire came from? Perhaps it grew out of all those years of silence."

He stared at his foot, and Todd wondered if that was the end of the story. What was he supposed to make of it all? That Peter Bennett was a noble and wonderful father? Or perhaps the story was really meant for Susan. Todd felt way out of his league. The titanic struggle, the monumental game of chess that Susan and her father played out, it was too fast and hard for him. The plot changes stretched his emotions one way, then another. Agonizing questions rose out of each move. Had Susan been lying about her birthday? Or perhaps just embellishing the truth? She never mentioned seeing psychiatrists. Then again, it was in the father's best interest to make it all sound different from Susan's account.

This story was engulfing him, swallowing him whole then dumping his tired soul in the middle of the Bennett maze. And all he could do was sit mutely and listen.

It was disconnecting him from his life, himself. A great weariness overcame him and his muscles started to ache from holding himself in the one position, too afraid to move in case he would attract attention.

Then Susan's father stood up, the audience over, and a sudden burst of energy filled the room. He held out his hand and said, "I'm sorry we had to meet under these circumstances, Todd."

Todd shook the meaty hand, the skin surprisingly rough, the grip strong. Then the man was gone, with a vague instruction for Todd to let himself out quietly when he went. When he was sure Susan's father had vanished, Todd went cautiously upstairs, knocking on Neat's door first. The room was empty, so he stood in the hallway, frozen with indecision. He didn't want to call out—that would attract attention. Knocking on any other door was fraught with danger; what if he knocked on her parents' door? He'd probably have to sit through another deep and meaningful with the father. Home was the only option, out onto the streets again to rely on the indifference of late-night public transport. His moment had passed; Susan was no doubt fast asleep somewhere.

Todd left, shutting the front door quietly after him as he had been instructed, then walking briskly down to the street. There was a cold snap in the air tonight, and he slapped his thighs in a vain attempt to get his blood running faster. He had no idea when the next bus would come, so he decided to walk.

He turned off the main road, following the bus route through the suburbs. The lights were out here, and a dark pall hung over the streets. It was as if a curtain had been dropped on a stage, or the arc lights suddenly dimmed—a dramatic end to the second act.

He hung his head low, as if that would keep the heat in or the cold out, and half-walked, half-ran home.

Susan

My back feels bent in at least three places. I have a sharp, vibrating pain on one side of my neck and a stray paper clip has managed to work itself up my T-shirt and lodge in my bra strap. I suppose this is how most people feel when they wake on their first morning after being saved. Of course, the fact that I slept the night curled up on my father's study floor might have something to do with it. My savior, my Neat, is still asleep, adrift on a makeshift bed, oblivious to the world, to my face, my spaghetti pain that he insists I eat. Could it be as simple as that? All I have to do is open my mouth and take it all in—all the crap and despair and loneliness of the past eight years? Last night it sounded exciting, tantalizing even. All my rough spots felt tickled by the prospect of Neat's recipe. This morning I just feel hungry, not to mention sore.

I open the door and sneak a look outside. My father's snoring reassures me that the coast is clear for the moment. As I make a quick dash downstairs for food, I wonder, do I feel saved? Is this the promise Neat has peddled on his TV show to the vagabonds who watch? I'd love to be able to say that the world is completely different this morning, that all I feel is love and compassion for my family, but that would be a bag of cow spit.

Yeah, I'm real saved, I'm the new Susan Bennett, sneaking into my kitchen so I don't wake up my father. Opening the door quietly, anything to avoid seeing him face to face. I'm the perfect model of the reformed bitch, too afraid to face the enemy because I know if I do I'll pounce. Sure, I swallowed last night, I cried and I "saw" Neat for the first time in ages, but it doesn't take away my struggle with Daddy dear. I don't think anything can do that.

The fridge is disappointingly barren. I grab whatever is vaguely edible, then sneak a look around. No sign of Todd; he must have left after the epic battle. I wouldn't be surprised if he never came back. Specially after I left him holding the parents, so to speak. Will he forgive me? Will he see that I had to do it, that walking out was life and death stuff for me? God, I felt so strong, breaking out of the argument like that, coming in to Neat, sitting down with him. Last night.

With a tray full of leftovers I lock myself in our hide-out. It's like a cubby in here, the room so dark, so secretive. I open the curtain and a brilliant splash of colored light flings itself across the bookshelf, leaking onto the wall. The morning sun, refracted by the expensive beveled glass of Father's window. I hold my hand in the rainbow light. So many colored moods—fiery, salty, serene, garish—innocent white light split into its many parts, never to be joined again. They are like the many colors of me. The red warrior-woman, the blue frightened child, the green sharp-tongued bitch from hell, and the pink blushing girl on the bus—each has her singular use, but they're not useful enough. Put them together, however, and they make the white light of me, Susan Bennett. Perhaps that is my salvation, to be able to join these colors. The gift of white light from my pale, fat brother.

He needs to eat, so do I. A stale piece of white bread, in the early stages of decay, beckons from the tray. As I munch, I realize that today is Saturday—*Fat Boy Saves World* day. I pause in my exploration of mold. For the first time since Neat's sorry piece of video garbage began, I see endless possibilities for its use. This could be a day that they will never forget down at community TV land.

Todd

He woke with a head as thick as a bucket of scum. All night he'd dreamed about his old farm, the wind blowing dust into his hair, his eyes, his clothes, his mouth, until he turned into dust. Heavy, dusty, cementlike body, trudging through the paddocks, stepping in all the cow pats, reeling from their sweet, grassy, gassy smell. Flicking off the wheat chaff that irritates his skin, the sun so hot and the air so stifling.

Todd sat on his thin foam mattress, his dusty dream vanishing fast. He should have felt light breezes blowing about his ears, should have heard the far-off call of livestock, the usual aftermath of his farm dreams. Instead he felt as though someone had taken a cricket bat and tried to flatten his forehead out. He drank from the glass beside his bed, the water old and metallic, trying to break down the cake of dryness that had lodged in his throat.

It must have been two in the morning by the time he'd collapsed into bed, his muscles aching from the cold air and the long walk. He thought he would fall asleep straightaway, but he lay awake, tossing fitfully, trying to make sense of all the madness that rattled about in his head. He must have slept eventually; otherwise where did the dreams come from?

He shuffled to the kitchen and rummaged around in the cupboards for a while until he found a small, red medicine box with "Rick's! Hand's Off!!" scrawled on the side. Not caring what his moody roommate Rick would think, Todd grabbed a couple of painkillers and swallowed them with fresh water before stumbling back to bed. He had to sleep more, try to shake off this horrible monster that insisted on squeezing his body and strangling him. The bed smelled sweaty and old, but he didn't mind. He lay down and listened to the drumbeat of pain in the front of his head.

Eventually he fell into a fitful sleep, feeling slightly better when he woke again. He looked at the clock. It was 1:54 PM, still time to get to Susan's before the show. He had no idea if she was going to Comm TV, or for that matter if Neat was going. He hoped the show was still happening, that Susan's father hadn't stopped it. He didn't want to lose "Fat Boy Saves World." Something had to survive out of all this mess.

The bus ride was a nightmare, crammed in between

hot bodies in the airless metal box. Todd was almost sick by the time he reached Susan's house, so he sat in the driveway for a while to settle his stomach. He thought he could hear a voice in the distance, calling, becoming louder. "Susan! Susan!" It was her father, coming down the driveway, crunching the gravel, pink-faced, looking like he was ready to bite the world in two. Todd allowed himself a private smile, because Peter Bennett was so like his daughter.

"Where is she?" he yelled.

Todd shrugged, indicating that he had no idea. So the war was on again, the overnight lull in proceedings just a rest stop on the highway to hell. "Do you know where this TV thing is?" asked Peter Bennett.

"Yes," said Todd. "I do."

"Well, Susan's taken Brian there. She locked herself in the bloody study all day, and now she's vanished. Would you take me there, Todd? It's very important."

Todd froze, knowing that Susan would want him to refuse, but he couldn't. He didn't want this anger turned on him.

"I'll get the car," said Susan's father, taking his silence as a yes, and Todd nodded like a cheap toy from the supermarket.

Susan

I'm a fugitive, a refugee, a freedom fighter holed up in a tiny peasant hut, trying to ignore Daddy's rantings outside in the hallway, his threats to call the police (as if they could do any good), his pleadings with Neat, his anger. During one of the lulls I look over at my brother sitting serenely against the wall.

"Why do you want to save the world?" I ask. It's as good a question as any in the circumstances.

He looks straight through me, as though he's seeing stuff way past the walls of the study, way past our garden, into God knows where.

"I'm not scared anymore," he answers.

That's the answer? I'm not scared? So, was he too afraid to save the world earlier? Or is fear the barrier that stops us from great things? No time to ponder the meaning—my father returns, says he wants to speak to me, tries to sound reasonable, but I won't fall for that trick. None of us will, none of the many Susans crammed into the room. The warrior-woman, our general, directing the resistance with ruthless authority and powerful camaraderie; the little Susan, who knows only too well what happens when you let Daddy in; the quick-witted Susan; the cynical Susan, the vulnerable Susan. So many parts, so many troops to keep the battlements strong. Eventually my father gives up on his reconciliatory approach and huffs off. The timing is perfect. Now is our chance to get out of here, down to the studio where the real work needs to be done.

I put my finger to my mouth and whisper "ssh" to Neat, but he stares at me blankly, as if to say, "What do you think I've been doing all these years?" A fit of giggles sneaks up on me, and I shove my fist into my mouth as I open the study door. A quick look reveals no surprises, so we hustle downstairs and escape through the kitchen door. Once we're out of the house I explode into laughter and Neat smiles at me. We make our way down to the main road where I hail a taxi to COMM TV.

It's a quick journey, and we arrive with time to spare. I slip the driver his fare, then push my whale of a brother out of the cab.

Finally we enter the COMM TV foyer, where we are instantly greeted by Phil.

"Didn't you get my messages?" he shrieks. "I phoned and phoned . . . I dropped around—the house looked empty . . . God. I wasn't sure if I'd have a show today or what."

"You might still get the 'what' today, Phil," I say.

He looks a bit nonplussed by this, but I haven't got time to explain.

"Shall we tell them the truth, Neat?" I ask as we enter the studio—brother, sister, and duck.

He barely gives a nod. All his attention is on Rosie, who is waiting on one of the couches, a worried look on her face. As soon as she sees Neat she jumps up and gasps, "What's wrong?"

"Nothing's wrong," I say. "Everything's okay."

I stand in the middle of the set, feeling very awkward. About fifteen to twenty onlookers are crammed into the tiny space, and I reckon about another thirty might be watching at home. Phil arrives with two microphones, one for himself and one for Neat. I tell Phil that I'll hold Neat's for him. Time zaps by now, and Phil is doing his rousing opening spiel. It lacks oomph today, the words are hollow and passionless: ". . . Brian Bennett, silent for so many years until one day he found a voice . . ."

If he ever lost it in the first place.

". . . no longer the silent boy. Now he's the fat boy . . ."

Ah, the fat boy—that mythical creation everyone wants to cling to.

". . . and now he's here to save the world."

The applause is about as deafening as you would expect from a small studio full of enthusiastic people. Phil looks over to where Neat should be standing, but it's me. He gives me a "go away now" look, but I ignore it. I take a breath for courage, but I can't exactly feel it flooding in. Hell, what I'm about to do breaks years and years of silence, but I'm not stopping now.

"I have come," I say, "to do the right thing. I have come to destroy the fat boy."

Neat

He wants to know: Why are they bothered by what she says? Are her words so terrible?

He thinks: They should look at the words spray-painted on the wall behind him. They are more powerful.

He sees: The tiny little camera sweating under the lights, working hard to understand. The people, all working hard to understand.

He wants to say: Don't work so hard.

He whispers to Rosie: "It's me, Brian."

And she nods furiously, the noise in the studio rising to a crescendo.

Todd

Susan's father backed a shining European car out of a garage and unlocked the passenger door. Todd climbed in mechanically, put his seat belt on, and said, "Head toward the city."

They didn't speak for the first few minutes, and Todd used this time to gather his thoughts. The last thing he wanted to do was show this man how to get to COMM TV so he could pull the plug on Neat's show. His leg started shaking involuntarily, all his anger and frustration manifest in the muscles. He hated sitting here like this, obeying orders, seeming to join in a conspiracy he would never support.

They turned onto the freeway ramp, a myriad of signs ahead of them, looming, warning of impending exits—left lane, right lane, straight ahead. . . So many choices. The city exit was ahead, the one they should take. They'd be at Comm TV in a few minutes. But there was a voice in Todd's ear, a whining mosquito, a nagging reminder of the prancing fool, Arlecchino. It whispered wicked thoughts to him, plotted devilish plots, laughed at the exciting turns they could make. Like the ring-road turnoff. It was next, a perfect diversion really, taking them far, far away from the city, from Comm TV. Todd nearly exploded with indecision. He had to do it, to listen to that wily trickster, for his own sake more than anything else.

"Take the ring road," said Todd.

Now he smiled; this was real action, this was his instinct speaking for the first time in days. His headache seemed to lift with the adrenaline rush, bringing relief.

"It's in the north, is it?" asked Peter Bennett, and Todd nodded, watching the inner-city streets recede to his left. No turning back now. Todd rubbed his hand along his thigh, trying to calm his nerves.

Peter Bennet kept glancing over at him. "You seem very tense," he said. "I'm sorry I shouted at you before. I was just so angry. Susan has taken Brian to the show. It was very irresponsible. Not that you'd agree with me. After all, it was your idea. Right?"

Todd had the good sense to nod his head. He knew what an expert questioner this man was—to enter into a conversation would be dangerous. On the other hand he couldn't grunt the entire way, it might arouse suspicions.

Peter Bennett opened the glove compartment, pulled out a packet of mints, carefully extracted one, and offered the packet to Todd.

"No thanks," said Todd automatically.

"They're not poisonous," said Susan's father. "At least I don't think they are. More stale than anything else."

"Mm," said Todd.

"You don't seem to be as talkative as you were last night, Todd."

"Nothing to talk about, is there?"

"Ah, so that's it. You've got me worked out. I'm the bad guy, riding into town to ruin everyone's fun. Is that it?"

"I dunno." Todd shrugged.

"Oh, come on. I already know that you're a bright fellow. You wouldn't be friends with Susan otherwise. So don't give me this noncommittal, teenage bull, okay?"

Todd gave the old guy the once-over. He was pretty perceptive. That remark about Susan was right on the money—she couldn't stand wishy-washy people.

"Okay," said Todd. "I do think you're gonna ruin everything, because you want to stop Neat's show. I mean, you haven't even seen it yet."

"That's true," said Peter Bennett thoughtfully. "But I have got Susan's description to go by. Exploitation."

"But it's not. I mean . . . it's nothing like that . . . not to the people who watch it. And besides, why would Susan take Neat to the show if she really thought it was exploitation?"

"Perhaps she intends putting an end to it too." Her father smiled. "She just wants to get in before I do."

Todd scratched his head furiously. The ins and outs and roundabouts of the Bennett minds were too much for him. He wanted it all kept simple, on terms he could easily understand. Why would Susan even bother to think like that? Because her father does? He sighed loudly, then wished he hadn't. The keen eye of Peter Bennett was on to him.

"You seem a bit frustrated by something, Todd."

He looked out the window, wondering how to avoid expanding on his sigh. They'd been traveling on the ring road for a few minutes now, and the scenery was looking more and more like the suburbs, places where you wouldn't find a TV studio. He would have to say something, to keep Susan's father talking, to divert his attention from their surroundings. Besides, he was sick of all this scheming. He longed for some straight talking.

"I don't get it," he said. "You said all this stuff to me last night about Susan . . . and it's like you understand her. But from what I can see, most of the time you're treating her like an arch enemy. She's your daughter. Why can't you say that stuff to her face?"

"I don't think she'd listen."

"How do you know? Have you tried it?"

"Oh, yes."

"When was the last time?"

Peter Bennett laughed. "I don't know. You're a terrier, aren't you? You don't give up."

"No, actually I'm a friend. So, no offense, but you go on about not violating Neat's trust and respecting his space . . . Well, what about Susan's trust, her space? You know, like, if you actually sat back and watched her for a few weeks like you watched Neat, you might see something different."

"If she'd let me."

Todd smiled. He could see where Susan got her barrier techniques from. Different style but same result. Everything he said was batted back at twice the speed.

"Something funny?" asked Peter Bennett.

"Doesn't matter," said Todd. "Can I ask you a question now?"

"Sure."

"Why aren't you proud that Neat wants to save the world?"

"Pardon?"

"I mean, he isn't saying, 'Give me more ice cream or

money' or whatever. He's saying, 'I want to save the world.'"

"Well, I don't know if he really understands what he means . . ."

"He does. I've seen it, believe me."

"Okay, you've seen it."

Todd felt his anger rising. There was something very frustrating about this man. He said all the right things about listening, but he didn't really listen at all.

They passed under a sign announcing that the ring road would end after one kilometer and Todd groaned inwardly. Any minute now Peter Bennett was going to realize he'd been had.

"Look, Todd," he said, "this might be a bit difficult to explain, but all through Brian's life he has been described by others, and I put myself at the forefront of that category. I described Brian in my book, gave him a literary code, if you like. He was the silent one, it was even the title of the book. It's a wonderful literary image, the silent child who won't speak because he is too troubled by the cares of the world. Highly romantic, evoking powerful emotions in the reader's heart and, I dare say, in Brian's as well. The trouble is, I think he's bought the whole persona. He's become the terribly noble silent witness who speaks for the first time, wanting to do good for the whole world."

Todd went over the words a few times to make sure he had the meaning right. Here was Neat's own father describing him as a character in a book. He didn't understand how anyone could think like that. Just seeing Neat with Rosie and Mr. Goodman was enough to convince him of the authenticity of the fat boy's intentions, his desire, his belief. It was real—extra real, if there was such a thing.

Then he realized that he'd made a terrible mistake, that for the past ten minutes he'd been leading Peter Bennett away from *Fat Boy Saves World,* when he should have been dragging him to that studio, demanding that he watch his son.

"It's all a bit complicated, wouldn't you agree, this life?" said Peter Bennett.

Todd agreed that the description of Neat was far too complicated, but as far as life went, he had other ideas. "No," he said. "I reckon life's pretty simple. You eat, you sleep, you have fun, you love people. And my dad would add one more thing to that: you don't tell lies."

Susan's father laughed. "Well, that certainly is simple."

"Do you want to hear something even funnier?" asked Todd.

"What?"

"I've been lying to you for the past ten minutes. We're nowhere near the TV station. I think you'd better turn the car around."

"Oh, hell!"

He turned the car around and headed back toward the city, his face set in fury. Todd closed his eyes, praying that he was doing the right thing. Peter Bennett's mad idea came back to him, that Susan might actually be trying to knock *Fat Boy Saves World* on the head herself, get in before her father. And a slight nut of doubt grew within him.

It was a long ten minutes. Peter Bennett, it would seem, was no longer in the mood for a philosophical chat. He parked illegally outside Comm TV, and hurried toward the foyer door.

"I'd like to say thanks for the directions, Todd," he said, "but I don't think I will."

They were late, the show was already running. He reached the studio door and had to push with all his strength to get it open. As he did so, he could hear a howl of voices coming from inside.

Too late, he thought, pushing his way in. Too bloody late.

Susan

Well, that was a good start, wasn't it? They loved my opening line about destroying the fat boy. I wait for a moment or two for the howl of protest to die down, but it doesn't, so I shout over the top of it.

"Hear me out. I'm his sister, and I'm here because I love him."

Now the volume subsides a little, and I seize this window of opportunity to continue my little speech.

"The fat boy is a fiction," I say (increase in the volume). "He was created first by fear and panic. The fat boy was created by my family. His silence, his story—we made it up. None of us knew we were doing it, we thought we were just loving him . . ."

The noise drowns me out in waves of protest. They don't seem to be getting my point. I'm trying to tell them about the past, about the way little rips turn into giant holes. About how a child can make a seemingly innocent choice in life that holds on for years and years and years. About how easy it is to turn someone who doesn't speak into what you want him to be. But the audience don't want to hear it. I need help, desperately. The assorted members of Neat's audience are starting to enter the set, shouting in my face, waving their soft toys at me. It must be time to give up, and I lower the microphone, only to feel it taken from my hand.

"Shut up!" I hear a voice yell.

It's Todd, his face red and angry. He's willing to give me another try, even after I deserted him. I feel like drowning the boy in my tears until he's sopping wet, so enormous is my relief. Then I see my father.

Todd calls for quiet once more, and the crowd responds slowly.

"Give her a chance," he yells. "If it wasn't for her, this show would never have started in the first place."

That's not exactly true, but I'm not going to quibble at the moment. There is a further, slight lowering of the roar, and Todd puts the microphone in my hand and says, "Are you okay?"

"I don't know, not with him here," I say, indicating my father, who is standing on the edge of the circle. He wants to come into the light and drag me out of there, but something seems to be stopping him. Must be his image; after all, he is a public figure. He won't risk being seen on community TV, especially when the chances are he'll be made to look foolish. That would be a disaster for him.

Todd leans even closer to me, his breath on my cheek, his sweet smell in the air I breathe.

"Susan," he whispers, softly, almost inaudibly, "what do you want?"

I'm startled by this question. I hadn't even bothered to think about what I want out of this. I've just been going with the flow, working on instinct. He'd approve of that, my theater boy, he'd say I was trusting in the drama. But what the hell will I do if the drama goes over the edge? Learn to fly, I suppose.

"I want the truth," I say.

He gives me a kiss on the cheek and says, "Go for it." For a moment the entire focus of my attention is on my cheek, then the urgent whisper of Phil in my ear snaps me out of it.

"Come on, this is boring."

Boring? How can life be boring? Certainly not in my family, anyway. I avoid my father's eyes and launch into the unknown.

"A friend once told me to listen for the truth in a story," I say. "That it might not always be what's obvious. So listen to this story. It's not boring. It's about the real fat boy, Brian Bennett."

Father has a smirk on his face. He's finding this amusing. You can't stop me, I chant to myself.

"The so-called fat boy is . . . he's an invention . . . a fiction. You invented him by coming here expecting answers from him. I invented him by turning him into a just cause, and others invented him by writing books about him."

Father's smirk has gone, I knew he wouldn't like the reference to The Book.

"Oh, Susan," he says, sounding so quiet among the clatter of the rabble.

Yes, it's Susan, your troublemaker, the one who won't shut up. I put my head up high and I swear to the god of shaven-headed young women that I will not turn away.

"I know you want to believe that my brother can swallow all your pain but he can't. Only you can."

Father shakes his head, shoulders slumped, and I miss the beat for a second. That's new. That's something I've never seen before. Is it his latest tactic? If it is, it's more effective than reaching in and grabbing the microphone from my hand.

"I think my brother has got answers . . . but you won't find them on this TV show . . . you'll find them on his face. What you've got to do is look at him. I know it sounds stupid . . . but just look at him because the real him . . . it's right there . . . his . . . his . . . Hell, I don't know what the right word is. His soul, I suppose." Everyone in the audience looks at Neat. But my gaze is on my father, who holds his head up. For a passing flash, as elusive as butterfly wings, he meets me. I nearly stumble, there on the yellow-glow set of *Fat Boy Saves World*. When did he learn to do that?

"Brian taught me something," I say, my voice going wobbly. Father is still looking, but differently now, from a safe distance. I continue. "Brian Bennett, not the fat boy or the silent boy, not creations or convenient myths. My brother taught me a powerful lesson these past few days."

How the hell do I explain this? With words, I suppose—those little ink blobs of truth. I take a deep breath. Here goes.

"Have you ever touched someone and felt a zap run through your arm like electricity? Have you ever caught a light in a friend's smile that's blown you away? Have you ever seen a little kid's face after they've stopped crying? I mean . . . whatever name you give to that overwhelming essence, it's always there. Look at us—we spend all our lives trying to cover it up with crap like anger and being cool and stuff. That's what he's trying to tell you—it doesn't go away, so grab hold of whatever it is that makes you remember that essence. Whatever it is that makes you feel how it felt when you were free of the bullshit."

I go to Neat and take Mr. D from his lap. "This is what did it for me," I say, holding up the duck.

They smile, the mad, hostile mob actually smile. They all have their own little cuddler tucked away under an arm or in a bag. They retrieve them now, and I burst out laughing. It is so magical, the look on their faces. They are transformed into row upon row of little children, hugging their bears in the middle of the cold, dark night. Nothing can touch them.

They storm onto the set, waving their little friends, and I'm swamped. The crowd pushes me off my spot, and when I look up, there is Father, his eyes on Mr. D.

"There's magic in this duck, Dad," I say, and he looks a little scared.

Phil hustles the rabble off the set, muttering about running out of time. "And we haven't even heard from the fat kid yet."

I hold the microphone up again, ready to continue, but a large, hot paw taps me on the shoulder, and a familiar rumble tickles my ear.

"It's my turn now, Susan," says Brian Bennett, brother bear, so I pass the duck and the microphone on to him and sit down, exhausted.

I can only see the back of my brother from here, fringed by studio light. He is saying something about the duck, but I can't concentrate. My father isn't watching Neat, his eyes are on me, and I do a little bow. He half smiles, nods his head a little, then looks quickly at his son, a sort of embarrassed gesture. I don't feel embarrassed. I feel raw, exposed, and a bit cheated. I want to rush out of the set, grab Dad, and say, "Don't look into the very heart of me unless you mean it, unless you've got the guts to keep looking." But who the hell would I be kidding? Do I have the guts to keep connected with him? I don't know. I'm too tired to work it out.

Neat is still talking, asking the crowd a question. They all have their hands up, all except for my father. Now my brother is leaving the set, he's holding out Mr. D to Dad, arm out straight, the duck almost quivering. What exactly is Neat offering here? It's more than a duck, I can tell you. Mr. D was always more than just a duck. He's offering our private communion, our giggles under the sheet, our nighttime voyages on the barge of dreams. He's saying, "Take them now if you want, so you never have to burst through bedroom doors to take them." I have this weird feeling that I'm the one who should be offering Mr. D, not Neat.

Father won't look at the duck, won't even meet Neat's gaze.

God, this is so important, this gift, this offering.

He must take it—surely he can see that—he must.

But he doesn't move.

Neat

They are so noisy. Can't they tell that Susan is telling a story?

He would like to listen because Susan is a good storyteller. She can make up fantastic voyages when she wants to.

He likes the way Susan is talking to everyone on his show.

He likes sitting next to Rosie. He likes the feel of her next to him.

He liked it when Todd told them to shut up.

He likes the fact that the noise is there but it is outside him now.

He tries to listen above the noise, to the story about Brian Bennett, to the words about the silent fat boy. He shrugs.

That might be what happened, who cares? He certainly doesn't anymore, not right here, right now. Why would he? Rosie doesn't care, not right here, right now. Why would she?

Now everyone wants to show off their soft friend, and he gets up slowly. It's time he talked to them. Besides, Susan is hogging the party.

He takes his duck, he takes the loud microphone.

"He's a duck," he says, microphone in one hand, Mr. D in the other. "When you hold him this way he looks like a dying man. See? And when you hold him that way he looks like a sleepy little girl. And when you hold him just so, he looks like a friend who hides her face in a book. And when I hold him to my ear . . . he's a duck again. He doesn't say quack. But he says an awful lot. He says he likes you . . . all of you. You're noisy, but he likes you. He'll tell you that to your ear if you want to listen. Who needs to talk to Mr. D?"

They put their hands up. Lots of them. Bright faces. Smiles, eager, except for one.

A very sour face, a loner. Yes, he's the one who needs a chat with Mr. D.

This face, this Daddy, he should hold Mr. D, he should listen. It might help rub out the fury of scribbles that spins around his head.

"Here you are," says Brian Bennett, walking into the gloom, holding the little yellow toy to his father. "Hold this duck."

Todd

Todd looked at Susan's father and waited. Would he take the duck?

Peter Bennett had surprised Todd so far, the way he handled his daughter's public confession—standing back, watching, even making eye contact with Susan.

Todd was sure this was the result of their car conversation, that the author had decided to give Susan the respect, the space that he'd shown his son. He just hoped that some good would come out of it now.

Susan had said she wanted to see the truth come out. The truth, it was something Todd berated himself for not seeing all along. If he'd been watching for the truth last night he would never have doubted Susan's motives. And what if her father watched for the truth right now, in this studio? Perhaps he could see Susan the way Todd saw her—alive, electric and warm. Perhaps Susan could see the truth in her father too—his love for Neat, his love for her, his tiny shred of willingness to listen to her, displayed in the way he stood back in the gloom. Wouldn't that be so simple? thought Todd.

And now Neat was offering the duck to Susan's father. A gift of love perhaps? He held his breath with her, watching Peter Bennett; he paused in empathy, in chorus with her desire, and waited.

Susan

The weirdest thing happens—the whole studio goes dead quiet. Even though mouths move around me, animated faces turn from Father to me, I can't hear a sound. And I won't, not until he acts. The studio floor seems to lift and lurch forward, and I push back with the balls of my feet. Don't go under, don't spin out, keep your stomach still and wait.

Father shrugs, giving Neat a silly smile, a tiny shake of the head. "Brian . . . not here . . ."

But Neat insists, the grubby duck squeezed tightly in his meaty hand, the offering. Surely Dad can see what's being presented to him. I will him to see it, to take the duck. He glances briefly at me, and we connect again, like a flash of lightning, then it's gone. He shakes his head in a gesture of finality, then turns and walks out of the studio.

Suddenly the scene erupts with noise, the volume knob nudged up to full.

I want to call out to him, but the mayhem and chaos overtake me. I should have known he couldn't do it. It was too much to ask for. The sight of his tall form weaving through the small crowd with their teddies and soft toys is the saddest thing I've ever seen.

Phil does the wrap now, a rousing description of today's wondrous show. God only knows what he made of all the Bennett angst.

Neat is holding Mr. D up next to his cheek, and they seem to have identical expressions on their faces. I put my arms around my brother and hold him.

"We'll get him," I whisper in Neat's ear. "We'll get Daddy to take our duck."

"No, Susan," he says, stepping back from my embrace.

No? What does he mean? Is he giving up? Neat hands the duck to me, and the meaning suddenly becomes clear.

"Okay," I say, taking Mr. D. "I know what to do."

This time my brother embraces me, and I nearly squeal with delight.

Neat

A warm hand sneaks the tiniest of squeezes on his arm, in the middle of his sister's hug, in the middle of the back pats. He looks at the duck in her hands, did it come from Mr. D? No, not this time.

When his sister has pulled away, he goes exploring, trying to find the owner of that squeeze. But he needn't have looked far, and he needn't have been amazed by the result of his search.

"Rosie, hello." He smiles, and she smiles too. "Would you like to come and visit a friend with me?"

She nods, and they quietly leave, the big boy and the big girl, on their way to a hospital to seek out an old man who knows how to ask questions.

And that is plenty.

Todd

The party of hangers-on milled around for some more action, even though the show was over. Susan caught Todd's eye from the middle of the crush and smiled, still busy with her brother.

Todd made his way toward her, and she disentangled herself to meet him, to hold him in a full embrace, to stay in there until he felt embarrassed, until he chuckled.

"What?" she asked.

"Nothing." He smiled. "I liked it. So, what are you going to call the show now? *Fat Boy and Bald Girl Save World?*"

"More like *Fat Boy and Bald Girl Confuse World.*"
Susan laughed. "Thanks for the advice and the kiss. It
helped a lot."

"All part of the service."

"There's something I've got to do. It may take a
while."

"No problem. I've got all night."

"But I need to do it alone."

He tried not to look disappointed and failed.

"Don't be like that," she said. "I'll call you."

"Sure. Okay."

"Todd!"

"You'll call. I believe you."

The bus ride home took almost an hour and he was
exhausted by the time he crawled into his foam bed.
He realized as he lay down that he didn't expect to
hear from her that night Then he noticed that his
lousy, flulike symptoms of the morning had almost
vanished.

"Psychosomatic." He grinned, and closed his eyes.

But sleep wouldn't come—there were too many
things to digest, so he went into the kitchen and did the
unthinkable. He washed the enormous stack of dishes.
When he'd finished he wiped down all the benches and
washed the cupboards. His housemates would probably
faint at the sight in the morning, if their eyes were open
wide enough. He contemplated cleaning more of the
house but thought better of it. On his way back to bed
he saw the envelope with the drama school logo.

"Shit," he muttered. He didn't know if he had the
strength to read their decision. But he had to, so he

ripped it open and read quickly, the words flashing into his brain.

"... pleased to inform you . . . successful . . . contact us as soon as possible . . ."

He felt no emotion as he read. No joy, no relief, nothing. Then a noise jangled his senses. The phone was ringing, and he rushed to answer it.

"Hello," came her familiar voice. "Got your bathing suit?"

Todd laughed, then punched the air. "Yes!"

Susan

I wonder if he's still sitting where I left him, in his study, comfortable in his favorite chair. He'll have a slightly bemused expression on his face, just a slight hint of emotion around the edges, breaking through the artificial tan he's obviously picked up in a hotel somewhere in Europe. I wonder if he's holding the present I left in his lap, or if he's staring at it. It isn't complicated. Nothing is, really.

It's as simple as the words I used when I placed the present in his lap. "This is for you, Dad."

He picked up my present, Mr. D, and asked, "What's this for?"

"A peace offering," I said.

"So, we're still at war?"

My immediate urge was to bite back at him—to play the game—but I didn't. I asked him a question, instead. "Remember those stories I wrote? You know, I won that prize for them."

"Yes," he said. "You showed promise."

Oh, he was testing me, I can tell you. "Promise" indeed! The old me was ready to tell him they were all plagiarized, to slap him in the face with that little detail. It would have been so easy. Yes, easy and true, but not the truth. Not the real meaning behind why I wrote them.

"I was trying to impress you. Did you know that? I wanted you to think ... I don't know. That I was clever ... or something."

"Well, I was impressed," he said.

"Thank you."

We were awkward after that. Hell, it wasn't too often we'd gone down this path. Usually we're trading punches. Mom poked her head in and paused at the sight of us.

"Well, you two all right, then?" she asked, as if she couldn't believe we weren't fighting.

"Yes," said Dad.

"Okay, then." She smiled. "I'm off to bed."

I called out to her. "Mom?"

"Yes?"

"Sorry about all that stuff ... your ashtray and sculptures ..."

"Yes, so am I."

"I think I know how to get them back ... at least ... they're with Verena."

"Verena!"

"So, I'll find out where she is if you like."

"Well, good," said Mom, a bit shocked. Then, softer, "That would be great, dear. Night." And she went off to bed.

Dad leaned back in his chair, the duck relegated to the desktop.

"Do you really have no idea why I gave you that duck?" I ask. "Why Neat wanted to give it to you?"

"Not really. . ."

"And you're the author." I laughed. "It's a symbol, for crying out loud. It represents. . ."

I couldn't do it. I couldn't bring myself to say the "L" word. I let the sentence hang, and Father smiled.

"I think I get the point," he said. "Do you want a drink?"

"No . . . thanks. I've got a phone call to make."

I left then. Todd would say it was the right dramatic moment to go. Me? I just couldn't handle any more closeness with my father. I suppose I'm taking little steps at the moment, at least where Dad is concerned.

Out here in the cool, dark night, the moon has gone into its shell, hiding behind some invisible black cloud. I've never seen anything romantic in the moon—it's just a lump of rock, spinning in a predictable orbit, behaving as it should, illuminating according to the charts.

I want far more exciting and adventurous symbols for my love. Ones that will spring forth with danger, that will dance on the edge of safety, will challenge and shake and roar. Find me one of those and I'll follow it.

So for now I'll have to settle for what is becoming a bit of a Saturday night ritual. I slip my jeans off and leave them sprawled on the side of the harbor pool, like a fallen down drunk. I pull my T-shirt off and toss it onto my shoes. Now I slip into the almost very cold water and shriek. A wicked laugh warns me that I'm about to be attacked, and I search in the semidark for his white body. It comes like a flash—lightning, quicksilver, a non-moon spirit—Todd. This time I go down quickly to the soft bottom, grabbing the sand in my hands, squeezing it between my toes, gripping the harbor floor, holding on. He'll come, that's an absolute certainty, he'll touch me and stroke my cold, cold head. It won't take long, here in the silent dark waters.

And when he arrives, when I feel his warm hand on my back, I will laugh in a hail of bubbles and mayhem.

I will scream—a long, silent roar.

9 781442 431058